PENGUIN BOOKS

THE GIRL IN BLUE

P. G. Wodehouse was born in Guildford in 1881 and educated at Dulwich College. After working for the Hong Kong and Shanghai Bank for two years, he left to earn his living as a journalist and storywriter, writing the 'By the Way' column in the old *Globe*. He also contributed a series of school stories to a magazine for boys, the *Captain*, in one of which Psmith made his first appearance. Going to America before the First World War, he sold a serial to the *Saturday Evening Post* and for the next twenty-five years almost all his books appeared first in this magazine. He was part author and writer of the lyrics of eighteen musical comedies including *Kissing Time*; he married in 1914 and in 1955 took American citizenship. He wrote over ninety books and his work has won world-wide acclaim, being translated into many languages. *The Times* hailed him as a 'comic genius recognized in his lifetime as a classic and an old master of farce'.

P. G. Wodehouse said, 'I believe there are two ways of writing novels. One is mine, making a sort of musical comedy without music and ignoring real life altogether; the other is going right deep down into life and not caring a damn . . .' He was created a Knight of the British Empire in the New Year's Honours List in 1975. In a BBC interview he said that he had no ambitions left, now that he had been knighted and there was a waxwork of him in Madame Tussauds. He died on St Valentine's Day in 1975 at the age of ninety-three.

P. G. WODEHOUSE

The Girl in Blue

PENGUIN BOOKS

PENGUIN BOOKS

Published by the Penguin Group
27 Wrights Lane, London w8 5tz, England
Viking Penguin Inc., 40 West 23rd Street, New York, New York 10010, USA
Penguin Books Australia Ltd, Ringwood, Victoria, Australia
Penguin Books Canada Ltd, 2801 John Street, Markham, Ontario, Canada l3r 1b4
Penguin Books (NZ) Ltd, 182–190 Wairau Road, Auckland 10, New Zealand

Penguin Books Ltd, Registered Offices: Harmondsworth, Middlesex, England

First published by Barrie & Jenkins 1970
Published in Penguin Books 1987
Reprinted 1988

Reproduced, printed and bound in Great Britain by
Hazell Watson & Viney Limited
Member of BPCC plc
Aylesbury Bucks
Typeset in Baskerville

Chapter One

The afternoon sun poured brightly into the office of the
manager of Guildenstern's Stores, Madison Avenue,
New York, but there was no corresponding sunshine in
the heart of Homer Pyle, the eminent corporation
lawyer, as he sat there. He had in the opinion of his
companion in the room something of the uneasy air of
a cat on hot bricks. Nor is it difficult to probe the reason
for his loss of aplomb. A good corporation lawyer can
generally take it as well as dish it out, but it is trying
him too high when you telephone him in the middle of
the day's work to inform him that his sister has just
been arrested for shoplifting. In similar circumstances
a Justice of the Supreme Court would wriggle and
perspire.

It added to Homer's discomfort that he was being
interviewed not by the manager, an old college friend
from whom he could have expected sympathy and
consideration, but by one of those sleek, shiny young
men managers collect about them, the sort of young man
whom he himself might have employed in his Wall
Street office as a junior clerk. And from this stripling's
manner sympathy and consideration were markedly
absent.

He dabbed at his forehead with his handkerchief. He
had a large, round face, mostly horn-rimmed spectacles,
and its pores opened readily when he was agitated.

'There must be some mistake,' he said.

'Yup,' said the shiny young man. 'She made it.'

'Mrs. Clayborne is a wealthy woman.'

'Why wouldn't she be, when her shopping costs her nothing?'

'Why should she purloin goods from a department store?'

'Search me. All I know is we caught her with them.'

'It must have been a prank. She did it on a sudden impulse, just to see if she could do it.'

'And she found out she couldn't.'

The thought may have occurred to Homer that the shiny young man, like Jean Kerr's snake, was having all the lines and that he himself was merely playing straight for him, for at this point he relapsed into a sombre silence. He sat musing on his sister Bernadette. Hers, he had long been aware, was a nature which led her too often to act on impulse. There was the time when she had plunged into the Central Park lake in a form-fitting tweed dress from Tailored Woman to rescue a water-logged Pekinese, and that other time when she had beaten a tough egg into a scrambled egg with her umbrella for kicking a stray cat. More than most women she seldom gave a clue as to what she would be up to next.

But if one raised one's eyebrows at these and similar exercises in self-expression, at shoplifting one definitely pursed the lips. Here, one felt, she had gone too far. Not her fault, of course. It was, he supposed, a sort of mental illness. Paradoxically, she helped herself because she could not help herself. Their mutual aunt Betsy, now deceased, had suffered in the same way and had come to grief during the Autumn sales at Gimbel's. It had been until today the great scandal in the family.

The shiny young man was speaking again, this time on a more cheerful note.

'The boss says to tell you he won't prefer charges.'

This evidence that the old college spirit still lingered in the bosom of the man up top caused an immediate improvement in Homer's morale. It meant that there was going to be no publicity, and it was the thought of publicity that had burned into his soul like an acid.

'Provided,' the speaker continued, and the world became dark again.

'Provided?' he quavered.

'Provided you get her out of the city right away.'

Homer's sigh of relief was virtually a snort.

'That can be managed.'

'It better be.'

'I mean,' Homer explained with a dignity he could not have achieved five minutes earlier, 'that I am leaving for Europe almost at once and can take Mrs. Clayborne with me. I am going to Brussels to attend the conference of the P.E.N.'

The effect of these words was sensational. The shiny young man drew his breath in sharply. A new light had come into his eyes, which until then had had the icy glare of a district attorney cross-examining a shifty witness.

'P.E.N.?' He seemed stunned. 'But you aren't a writer.'

'In my spare time I write occasional poetry.'

'You do? Well, I'll be darned. So do I.'

'I find it soothing.'

'Me, too. Keeps you from going loco in the rat race. Ever have any published?'

'A few in the smaller magazines.'

'Same here. They don't pay much.'

'No indeed.'

'What sort do you do?'

'Lyrical mainly.'

'Mine are mostly songs of protest.'

'I have never written a song of protest.'

'You ought to try one some time.'

The atmosphere in the manager's sanctum had now changed completely, and essentially for the better.

7

Homer, who had been regarding the shiny young man as a particularly noxious specimen of a younger generation with which he was never at his ease, took another look at him and immediately became aware of his many merits. The shiny young man, who had conceived at the outset an immediate distaste for Homer because he was so obviously rich—just, in fact, the sort of capitalist he wrote songs of protest about—saw in him now an unfortunate toad beneath the harrow who was more to be pitied than censured if his sisters kept getting pinched for shoplifting. The thing, in short, had taken on the quality of a love feast.

'Look,' said the shiny young man. No, away with evasion and circumlocution. His name was Duane Stottlemeyer, so let us call him Duane Stottlemeyer. 'Look,' said Duane Stottlemeyer, 'hasn't it struck you that it isn't all such plain sailing as you seem to think? Seems to me you're in a spot.'

'I do not understand you.'

'Well, look. You say you're going to Brussels.'

'Yes.'

'Taking the dame, I should say Mrs. Clayborne, with you?'

'Yes.'

'Lots of department stores in Brussels,' said Duane darkly.

He had no need to labour his point. Homer got it without difficulty, and his jaw fell a notch. One cannot think of everything, and he had not thought of that. The arresting of shoplifters, like Art, knows no frontiers. A repugnance towards those who lift shops is common to all emporia, whether in the United States of America or on the other side of the ocean. There rose before his eyes a picture of his sister Bernadette with a Belgian store detective attached to each arm and stolen goods dribbling out of all her pockets being hauled to the office of a manager who would not be an old college friend of his. It was a vision to daunt the stoutest brother. He stared at Duane Stottlemeyer, aghast.

'But what can I do?' he gasped, and Duane did not fail him.

'I'll tell you what I'd do if it was me,' he said. 'I wouldn't take her to Brussels.'

'Then what—?'

'I'd leave her in England. Not in London, naturally. That would be just asking for it.'

'Then where?'

'In one of those country houses where they take in paying guests. Plenty of them around these days. Matter of fact, there was an advertisement of one in the *New Yorker* only last week. A place of the name of Mellingham Hall. I happened to notice it because I'd heard a man I know speak of it when he was over here. Jerry West. English fellow. Came to play in the amateur golf championship. When he was in New York, he had a card for my club, and I saw a good deal of him. He said that if I was ever going across, I ought to stay at this place. An uncle of his runs it, a guy called Scrope. What's the matter? Does the name ring a bell?'

Homer's face had lit up, as far as his type of face, the suet pudding type, is capable of lighting up.

'The Scrope you mention is the brother of Willoughby Scrope, a London lawyer with whom I have been associated on several occasions. It all comes back to me. I remember now hearing Willoughby Scrope speak of his brother Crispin and this house of his. It is quite a historic place, I believe.'

'Not near any department stores?'

'No, a long distance from London. In the depths of the country.'

'Sounds just what you want.'

'It could not be better. Willoughby Scrope can make all the arrangements for me. I will telephone him tomorrow. I don't know how to thank you.'

9

'Just the Stottlemeyer service.'
'The what service?'
'My name is Stottlemeyer.'
'Oh, how do you do, Mr. Stottlemeyer.'
'How do you do,' said Duane.

Chapter Two

It was shortly after this beautiful friendship had sprung up between Homer Pyle and Duane Stottlemeyer, a friendship which was to lead to them exchanging cards at Christmas and sending each other copies of their poems, that a nice-looking young man with ginger hair made his appearance at London's Queen's Bench Division 3 Court in the Strand. This was Gerald Godfrey Francis West, the Jerry West of whom Duane had spoken, and he had not come, one hastens to say, to stand in the dock and answer criminal charges. He had been summoned for jury duty, a thing that might happen to the best of us, and was about to sit on a hard bench and diligently enquire and true presentment make, as the legal slang has it.

The jury took their places in the box; the official whose job it was to keep the court stuffy made it stuffier; and Jerry, gazing at the girl at the far end of the row in which he sat, became more convinced than ever that the odd illusion of having been struck on the frontal bone by an atom bomb, experienced by him on his initial glimpse of her, had been due to love at first sight. It happens that way sometimes. A's love for B, or for the matter of thats C's love for D, often requiring long months before it comes to the boil, can occasionally start functioning with the sudden abruptness of one of those explosions in a London Street which slay six. There seems to be no fixed rule.

She was a girl of trim and clean-cut appearance, the open air type. He could picture her poised on the high board at the swimming pool, about to make a dive so expert that it would scarcely ruffle the surface of the water. He could see her driving a golf ball two hundred yards down the middle, a practice to which he himself was greatly addicted. She was also, he thought, though as yet he could not true presentment make, good at tennis. Her hair was a sort of soft brown, her chin firm and rounded. She was too far away for him to note the colour of her eyes, but he knew instinctively that they were just the colour eyes ought to be.

Ironical, he reflected, that when the jury summons reached him he had cursed so peevishly. An artist by profession, specializing in comic cartoons, he liked, when not playing golf, to devote the day to the practice of his art, and it was just his luck, he had felt, that he was not a borough treasurer, a registered dentist, a gaoler's sub-officer or one of the Brethren of Trinity House, for these pampered pets of the System are for some reason exempted from jury duty. Had he known that the summoners were also summoning girls like this one, how different his reception of their invasion of his privacy would have been.

What he and she and ten other males and females who were not registered dentists had come to sit in judgment on was the case of Onapoulos and Onapoulos versus the Lincolnshire and Eastern Counties Glass Bottling Company, one of those dull disputes between business firms where counsel keep handing books to the Judge and asking His Lordship with the greatest respect to cast an eye on the passage marked in pencil on the right-hand page, upon which he immediately looks at the left-hand page. ('Who is this Mr. Jones? I have nothing about him in my notes.' 'Your lordship is looking at the wrong page. If your lordship would kindly look at the right-hand page instead of the left-hand page.' 'But why should I *not* look at the left-hand page?' 'Because, my lord, with great deference there is nothing there concerning this particular case.') The only thing that kept Jerry from finding the proceedings intolerably tedious was the fortunate circumstance that the Judge, the counsel for the defence and several others of those present had richly comic faces, if some of them could be called faces at all, and he was able to occupy himself by making sketches of them in his note-book.

Emil Onapoulos was being cross-examined now concerning a verbal agreement alleged to have been made on November the fourth of the previous year, and Jerry saw a set look come into the face of the girl he loved, as if witness's responses were not satisfying her. Once or twice she pursed her attractive lips and her attractive nose gave a meaningful twitch. She seemed to be saying to herself that if he expected to have the ladies and gentlemen of the jury with him, Emil would have to do better than this.

His admiration of her became intensified. Here plainly was a girl who had everything—not only good at golf, swimming and tennis, but one with solid brains who could sift and weigh evidence, a girl whose swift intelligence enabled her to understand what the hell all these cryptic blighters were talking about, a thing which he himself had long since given up hope of doing.

Ages passed. Suddenly with a start of surprise—he was putting the finishing touches to his sketch of counsel for the defence at the moment—he found that the lawyers had had their say and that the jury was being requested to retire and consider its verdict.

The foreman called the meeting to order, and the arbiters of the fate of two Onapouloses and probably dozens of glass bottlers, for these glass bottlers breed like rabbits, especially in Lincolnshire and the eastern counties, began to express their opinions.

As is customary on these occasions, they varied from the fairly fatuous to the completely fatuous. It was left to the girl to take command of the proceedings. In a clear, musical voice which sounded to Jerry like the song of birds in the shrubbery of some old-world garden at eventide she indicated the course a conscientious jury was morally bound to take.

She was, it appeared, one hundred per cent for the glass bottlers. If she had been the affectionate niece of one of the company's vice-presidents, she could not have been more definite in her views.

She swayed her hearers from the start, especially Jerry. To say that he followed her reasoning would be an overstatement, but he agreed with every word of it. A Daniel come to judgment, he was saying to himself. He had no shadow of a doubt about following her lead. What was good enough for her, he felt, was good enough for him. He was sorry for Johnny Halliday, the Onapoulos's counsel, who was a personal friend of his, but fiat justitia, ruat coelum, as the fellow said, and a barrister of Johnny's experience must long ago have learned the lesson that you can't win 'em all. Without hesitation he added his contribution to the unanimous vote, and the diligent enquirers filed back into court to bring the glass bottlers the glad news which would send them strewing roses—or possibly bottles—from their hats all over Lincolnshire and the eastern counties.

2

Except for the Gadarene swine, famous through the ages for their prowess at the short sprint, no group is quicker off the mark than a jury at long last released from bondage, and in the stampede for the door Jerry and the girl were swept apart. But he caught up with her in the street outside and opened the conversation with an ingratiating cough.

Too often when a devout lover has worshipped from afar and is afforded for the first time a close-up of the adored object there is a sense of disappointment on his part. Jerry had no such feeling. She had appealed to his depths at long range, and she appealed to them even more now that they were standing face to face. Her eyes, he saw as she turned, were a sort of brown with golden lights in them and absolutely perfect, as he had known they would be.

She greeted him as if he were an old friend.

'Oh, hullo. You were on the jury, weren't you?' she said, and it surprised and pleased Jerry that she should have remembered him. Yes, he said, he had been on the jury, adding that he had had no alternative.

'The summons told me not to hereof fail, and I wasn't taking any chances. I wonder what they do to you if you hereof fail.'

'I believe they get awfully annoyed.'

'Something lingering with boiling oil in it?'

'I shouldn't wonder.'

'Not that it could be much worse than having to sit through a trial like that one.'

'Were you bored?'

'Stiff.'

'Poor Mr. ... Poor Mr. what?'

'Poor Mr. West. Poor Mr. G. G. F. West! It is too bad it affected you like that. I enjoyed it myself. But I'm surprised that you should have been bored. You seemed so interested.'

'Me?'

'I saw you making notes very intently all the time in your note-book. I was tremendously impressed.'

'Not notes. Sketches. I was drawing the Judge and other freaks.'

'Are you an artist?'

'Sort of. Cartoons mostly.'

'Well, that's better than painting Russian princesses lying in the nude on tiger skins.'

'Why do you specify that?'

'It's what an aunt of mine who lives in Bournemouth

thinks artists do. What kind of cartoons? Comic?'

'They try to be.'

'Curious. I'm a comic cartoon aficianado, but I don't remember ever seeing one by G. G. F. West.'

'I sign them Jerry.'

'For heaven's sake! May I have your autograph, maître? I'm one of your greatest admirers.'

Jerry gulped to facilitate speech, of which this astounding revelation had momentarily deprived him. Resisting an urge to say that it seemed to draw them very close together, he substituted the weaker 'Oh, really?'

'You've cheered me up more often than you could shake a stick at. And in my line of business you need constant cheering up.'

'Why's that?'

'Too much smiling to do. Very lowering to the spirits. I'm an air hostess. And not only lowering to the spirits; extremely wearing on the cheek muscles.'

'Still, you must meet a lot of interesting people.'

'Why the still?'

'You spoke as if you didn't like the job.'

'Oh, I do. I like it a lot. One sees the great world and, as you say, one meets a lot of interesting people.' She laughed. Analysing it, Jerry described it to himself as a silvery laugh. Rather like, he thought, for there was a touch of the poet in him, the sound ice makes in a jug of beer on a hot day in August. 'I was thinking,' she explained, 'of an old man named Donahue who travelled with us a good deal and was always in a bad temper. "Girl!" he used to bellow at me, and he never failed to snarl at me like a wounded puma for not coming quick enough. Finally I told him the trouble was that he always seemed to catch me when I wasn't in my spiked shoes and running shorts, and after that we got on fine. Somebody told me just before I went on leave that he was dead. I was sorry. Oh yes, it's quite a pleasant life.'

'Of course, you really ought to be a barrister.'

'What makes you say that?'

'I was thinking of your summing up just now. You were extraordinarily lucid when addressing us. I was stunned by your eloquence. How did you get that way?'

'I did a lot of debating at school.'

'Roedean?'

'Cheltenham.'

'Good Lord, I was at Cheltenham myself. Not the girls' school, the other one.'

'What a shame we never met.'

'Well, we've met now.'

'We have indeed.'

'So how about a bite of lunch? No, sorry, I was forgetting. I've got to lunch with my trustee.'

'Have you a trustee? How grand.'

'How about dinner?'

'I shan't be here for dinner. I'm going to Bournemouth to stay with my aunt.'

'For long?'

'A few days.'

'So tomorrow won't be any good either?'

'I'm afraid not.'

'The day after tomorrow?'

'I doubt it.'

'The day after the day after tomorrow?'

'Still doubtful.'

'Then let's make it the day after the day after the day after tomorrow.'

'Where does that land us?'

'It's a Friday. I think.'

'That ought to be all right. Where?'

'Barribault's. Round about eight.'

'I'll be there.'

She hailed a passing taxi, and was gone, and as he stood there looking after her a passer-by might have observed a soft glow in his eyes, if passers-by do observe soft glows in people's eyes. Probably they do not, but it was there. He was dreaming an opalescent day dream. Previously he had seemed to see her on the high board, about to make a perfect dive. He now saw her in the office of a registrar licensed to perform marriages, for he was sure that a girl like that would not want one of those ghastly choral weddings with bishops and assistant clergy horsing about all over the place. They would get it all fixed up in a couple of minutes, and later on they would sit together in their cozy little nest like two love birds on a perch. In the long winter evenings that would be, of course. In the summer they would be playing golf or enjoying a refreshing swim.

It was as his mind's eye was probing even more deeply into their domestic life that there came to him the realization that there was an obstacle, and a rather serious one, in the way of the bliss he was contemplating. He had suddenly remembered, what for the moment had slipped his mind, that he was engaged to be married to someone else.

3

But even if he had not happened to recall this, his memory would have been refreshed a minute later, for as the taxi melted into the traffic a voice spoke his name, and pivoting on his axis with the disagreeable feeling that someone muscular had struck him in the solar plexus he perceived the Vera Upshaw to whom some weeks earlier he had plighted his troth.

She had just come up from the direction of Trafalgar Square, and many admirers of feminine beauty who were coming the other way had almost dislocated their necks looking after her. Nor could one reasonably blame them for these acrobatics. One felt that they had exercised laudable self-restraint in not whistling.

There are girls who are rather pretty and girls who

are all right: there are girls who aren't too bad and girls who have a certain something: but it is only seldom that one encounters a girl who is really spectacular and takes the breath away. Into this limited class Vera, only daughter of the late Charles ('Good old Charlie') Upshaw and his wife Dame Flora Faye, the actress, unquestionably fell.

She had started with every advantage. Her father, till he came out in spots from too much champagne, had been one of the handsomest men in London, and everyone with a liking for the theatre was familiar with the radiant loveliness of her mother. The only asset which she had not inherited from the latter was her velvet voice. Her own tended to be harsh.

There was harshness in it now, ignoring Jerry's 'Oh, hullo', she said 'Who was that?', and Jerry, who for some time had been vaguely conscious of something left undone, realized that he had omitted to ask his colleague of the jury box her name.

'I don't know her name. She was on the jury with me and we got talking after the show.'

'Oh,' said Vera, losing interest. 'Is that your best suit?' she continued, changing the subject. She had always been critical about his outer crust, for Jerry in the matter of clothes went in, as so many artists do, for the comfortable rather than the glamorous, and it was apparently her aim to convert him into what a songwriter earlier in the century once described as a specimen of the dressy men you meet up West. 'I should have thought you would have smartened up a little for the Savoy. Oh, well. When is your lunch?'

'One-thirty.'

'Then we've time to talk. Who will be there?'

'Just us chickens.'

'What on earth do you mean?'

'Nobody but Uncle Bill and me.'

'Then he must want to discuss the Trust.'

'I doubt it. He'll probably talk golf all the time.'

'You mustn't let him. This is your big chance. You must get that money out of him. You ought to have done it long ago.'

She spoke with the imperious curtness of a princess of the Middle Ages giving instructions to one of the scullions or scurvy knaves on her pay roll, and Jerry found himself regarding her with disfavour. Even before his soul mate had come into his life he had begun to entertain doubts as to whether in contracting to link his lot with that of Vera Upshaw he might not have been a little precipitate. It had seeemed a good idea at the time, but after a while something uncomfortably like regret had begun to creep in. Had it, he asked himself, been altogether wise to sign on the dotted line with one in whom the bossiness which too often goes with extreme beauty was so marked? Those lustrous eyes of hers, though admittedly like twin stars, could flash in a very disconcerting manner when she was displeased. And there was so much about him that seemed to displease her, notably his reluctance to badger his trustee about that damned money.

He curbed his irritation and tried to speak with his usual amiability.

'The trouble about getting anything out of Uncle Bill is that he's always kidding. You try to make him stick to the point, and he puts you off with a wisecrack or starts talking about that collection of his. It's difficult to pin him down.'

'You could do it if you tried.'

'I have tried.'

'Well, try again. We can't talk here,' said Vera petulantly as the third passer-by in two minutes bumped into her. 'Let's go to the Savoy and have a cocktail at the bar. What I can't understand,' she said as they sat with their drinks before them, 'is why your money should be in trust at all. Your father left it to you, so why didn't you just get it? Why all this nonsense about your not having it till you're thirty unless Mr. Scrope releases it?'

'I explained that,' said Jerry, and indeed he had done so on more than one occasion, but either her memory was as treacherous as his own or, like the deaf adder in Holy Writ, she was a bad listener. 'I have it from Uncle Bill that Father was a total loss as a young man, couldn't settle to anything, couldn't save any money, couldn't get out of debt, just drifted. Then when he was thirty everything suddenly changed. I think he must have had one of those religious conversions you read about. He married, settled down, got a job, stuck to it, saved money, and then went into business for himself and was a big success. And that apparently gave him the idea that no man amounted to anything till he was thirty and wasn't to be trusted with money till then.'

'Utterly ridiculous.'

'I've always thought so, too. But I wasn't consulted. So I've three more years to wait.'

'No, you haven't.'

'Surely? Thirty is the magic number, and I'm twenty-seven.'

'There's no earthly need for you to wait three years. I've seen a lawyer about it. He says it all depends on whether the trust is perpetual and irrevocable, and yours can't be, because Mr. Scrope can give you the money whenever he likes. So you examine what they call the original indentures, just to make sure, and then you draw up a summons and complaint and have them served, demanding the termination of the trust. So you tell Mr. Scrope at lunch today that that's what you're going to do.'

'Oh, golly!'

'I shall be furious if you don't.'

Jerry nodded unhappily. He could well believe her.

Chapter Three

While Jerry and his colleagues were deciding the fate of the East Lincolnshire glass bottlers in Queen's Bench Division 3, business had been proceeding as usual at the offices of Scrope, Ashby and Pemberton in Bedford Row.

The days when London lawyers conducted their affairs in dark and depressing dens have long been past, for the modern lawyer likes his comforts and feels that the best is none too good for him. The premises of Scrope, Ashby and Pemberton were bright, airy and tastefully furnished, and their waiting-room was rendered additionally attractive by the presence there of a receptionist with an hour-glass figure and a good deal of golden hair. She reminded the caller who had just crossed the threshold of barmaids he had known in his youth, when barmaids had entered rather largely into his life. He approached her desk nervously, for circumstances had made him a nervous man. He had to clear his throat before he could speak, and when he spoke he spoke humbly.

'Could I see Mr. Scrope?'

'What name, sir?'

'Mr. Scrope.'

'Your name, sir.'

'Mr. Scrope.'

'Mr. Scrope?'

'Mr. Crispin Scrope. I am Mr. Scrope's brother.'

'Oh, I beg your pardon, Mr. Scrope. Mr. Scrope is

engaged at the moment, Mr. Scrope. Will you take a seat, Mr. Scrope.'

Mr. Scrope took a seat and settled himself to wait till Mr. Scrope should find himself at liberty. He was an elderly man with thinning hair, watery blue eyes and a drooping moustache, and he was wearing the anxious look so often seen on the faces of elderly men with thinning hair when they are about to try to borrow money from their younger brothers. From time to time a twitching shudder ran through his gaunt frame. The recent exchanges on the subject of Scropes had robbed him of the little confidence he had possessed when starting out on his mission, and the longer he sat, the less did it seem to him probable that his brother Willoughby, good fellow though he was and kindly disposed though he had shown himself in the past to applications for loans on a smaller scale, could be relied on for the stupendous one of two hundred and three pounds six shillings and fourpence—a sum roughly equivalent, or so it appeared to Crispin's fevered mind, to what it costs to put a man on the moon.

Time limped by, and he was just thinking that if he had any sense, he would have sent his brother a telegram arranging a meeting elsewhere instead of calling without notice in the middle of a busy morning, when the door with the legend 'Willoughby Scrope' on it opened, and a large, prosperous-looking man appeared, ushering out another large, prosperous-looking man. Hands were shaken, the visitor went on his way, and the first large, prosperous-looking man turned to the receptionist.

'I beat him hollow, Mabel.'

'I beg your pardon, Mr. Scrope?'

'Putting into a tooth glass. He was corn before my sickle. My score was twenty-three, his a meagre eleven.'

'Congratulations, Mr. Scrope.'

'Well earned, though I say it myself. Do you know

what the secret of successful putting is, Mabel? Perfect co-ordination of hand and eye, and to obtain these the stance must be right, not too rigid, but at the same time not too limp.' Willoughby Scrope turned to the visitor. 'You agree with me, sir?' he said, and paused, staring. 'For heaven's sake! Crips!'

'Hullo, Bill.'

There is generally a physical resemblance, if only slightly, between brothers, but it was hard to believe that these two were so related. Crispin was thin and diffident; Willoughby plump and exuding the self-confidence which comes with success. Crispin looked the typical poor relation, Willoughby obviously the rich one. Nor would anyone who so classified them have been in error. Willoughby had one of the most lucrative practises in London, while all that Fate had allotted to Crispin was a large country house with insufficient money to maintain it. The Scropes of Mellingham Hall had functioned more than comfortably through a number of centuries, but the present owner of that ancient pile, as he often said, did not know which way to turn, all he had to console him was the memory of the costly fun he had enjoyed in his youth. Willoughby, the younger son, who after the fashion of younger sons had been thrust out into the world to earn his living, was now in the highest income tax bracket: Crispin, the heir, was forced to take in paying guests in order to make both ends meet: and now there was yawning between those ends a gap of two hundred and three pounds six shillings and fourpence.

Willoughby was still staring. A visit from his brother was the last thing he had been expecting. He had always accepted it as one of the facts of life that Crispin never came to London. Negotiations for those small loans of which mention was made earlier had always been conducted over the telephone.

'I didn't know you were here, Crips. Why didn't you

tell me, Mabel?'

'I assumed you would not wish to be interrupted while you were in conference, Mr. Scrope,' said the receptionist with a dignity that became her well, and Willoughby had to admit that this was a proper spirit.

'Quite right. It would have interfered with the perfect co-ordination of hand and eye. Well, come along in, Crips,' said Willoughby, and Crispin, as he followed him into his office, was conscious of a faint but distinct thrill of hope. Bill, it was plain, was in merry mood this morning. Whether it was merry enough to make him write a cheque for two hundred and three pounds, six shillings and fourpence only time would tell, but the omens seemed favourable.

In the office there was no diminution of Willoughby's exuberance. He was all bounce and effervescence. He hummed little snatches of song, he skipped rather than walked. If there was a sunnier lawyer in Bedford Row that morning, he would have been hard to find.

'Fancy you bobbing up, Crips. Have a cigar?'

'No, thank you, Bill.'

'You'll lunch, of course?'

'I'm sorry. I have to catch the one-fifteen.'

'Pity. I'm giving Jerry lunch at the Savoy. He would have liked to see you.'

Crispin welcomed the opportunity to postpone for a few minutes the subject of loans and cheques. Eager though he was to discuss the main item on the agenda paper, at the same time he shrank from bringing it up. This, a familiar attitude with cats in adages, is also almost universal among diffident men trying to key themselves up to asking for large sums of money. One might put it that they let 'I dare not' wait upon 'I would'.

'How is Jerry these days?' he asked.

'Seems pretty fit.'

'How's he doing?'

'All right, I imagine. I haven't heard any complaints.'

'Have you let him have that money his father left him?'

'No.'

'I think you ought to, Bill.'

Crispin spoke with feeling. He knew that the sum in question was a substantial one, for the late Joseph West had done well manufacturing chinaware up North, and Jerry was a young fellow with a kindly heart, who, if in possession of a large bank account, could be relied on to do the right thing by an impecunious uncle.

'Why don't you, Bill? I know he's got his work and you give him an allowance of a sort, but a man of Jerry's age ... what is he now? Twenty-six? Twenty-seven? ... ought to have capital. He might want to do all sorts of things with it.'

'You never said a truer word. To start with he'd marry that Upshaw female he's gone and got engaged to.'

'I didn't know he was engaged.'

'A girl called Vera Upshaw.'

'Any connection of Charlie Upshaw?'

'His daughter.'

'I used to know Charlie rather well years ago. Before he died, of course. Didn't he marry Flora Faye?'

'He did.'

'Is the daughter on the stage?'

'No. She writes. Not the sort of stuff I like, but I believe many people do. Slim volumes with titles like Daffodil Days and Morning's At Seven. Whimsical essays.'

'Good God.'

'Yes, that's how I feel, too, but that isn't the reason why I don't want Jerry to marry her.'

'Why don't you?'

'Because she's utterly wrong for him. Do you remember that second breach of promise case of yours?'

A quick blink of Crispin's mild eyes showed that that

unfortunate episode of the days when he had been a well-heeled young man about town was still green in his memory.

'Why bring that up, Bill?' he asked reproachfully. He liked the dead past to bury its dead.

'Vera Upshaw reminds me of the girl who soaked you so much on that occasion. The same type. Lovely as an angel, but as hard as nails and sedulously on the make. All she wants is Jerry's money, or rather the money she's found out he's going to get some day.'

'How do you know?'

'She said so. She told him definitely that she wasn't going to marry him till I coughed up his capital. Which is why I'm not coughing it up.'

This evidence that his brother was not lightly to be parted from cash in his possession lowered Crispin's spirits, which at one time had tended to rise, and he sat chewing his moustache. Willoughby took advantage of this lull in the conversation to abandon the topic of G. G. F. West and his amours.

'But let's talk of something else,' he said, 'beginning with what brings you up here like this, when it's unheard of for you to come to London. Is it business?'

'No, not exactly business, Bill.'

'Income tax?'

'No, not income tax.'

'Something wrong at Mellingham? Trouble with the lodgers?'

'I wish you would not call them lodgers.'

'They lodge, don't they?'

'Yes, curse them.'

'Well, then. By the way, you aren't full up, are you?'

'No. Two of them left last week. Said they found it too quiet.'

'Then that's all right, because I'm sending you an addition to the menagerie. An American woman called Clayborne. Bernadette Clayborne, commonly known as

Barney. She's the sister of Homer Pyle, a New York lawyer I've occasionally worked with. Homer brought her over a couple of days ago, and they've been staying with me. He wants a quiet retreat for her in the country, and he made a point of it being a good way from London. Mellingham ought just to suit her.'

So bitterly had Crispin spoken of the two paying guests who had defected, thus depriving him of much-needed rent, that one would have supposed that he would have received this announcement with joyous enthusiasm. Instead, he was plainly stunned, and expressed his dismay with a batlike squeak.

'But I don't want women at Mellingham!'

'Of course you do. Home isn't home without the feminine touch.'

'She'll expect breakfast in bed.'

'Not Barney Clayborne. She's the kind of woman who goes for a five-mile walk before breakfast to get up an appetite. How well do you know your Chaucer?'

'My what?'

'The father of English poetry.'

'Oh, that Chaucer?'

'That's the one. Have you studied him lately? I ask because, if so, she will remind you of the Wife of Bath. You know the sort of thing—bright, breezy and full of beans.'

'My God! *Hearty?*'

'Yes, I suppose you would call her hearty.'

'I won't have her near Mellingham!'

'Think well, Crips.'

'I won't!'

'Your mind is made up?'

'Yes, it is. You don't understand, Bill. You're a big, beefy chap, and you don't know what it is to have sensitive nerves. A hearty woman would drive me insane.'

'Well, it's a pity, for she would have been paying

double your usual rates. Homer is loaded with money, and he's got to get his sister settled before he leaves for Brussels. He's a member of P.E.N. and he has to attend the conference they're having there, so I was able to make the terms stiff.'

For a moment or two Crispin sat plunged in thought. Then he said, 'Oh', and the monosyllable indicated clearly that his iron front had crumbled beneath the impact of second thoughts. He said All right, the woman could come, but there was no elation in his voice, and he went on to put into words his sentiments concerning those who enjoyed the hospitality of Mellingham Hall.

'Curse and damn all paying guests! And curse Mellingham! I wish I could sell the foul place.'

'Why don't you?'

Crispin uttered a laugh of the variety usually called mirthless, and Willoughby regarded him with some concern.

'Your asthma bothering you again?'

'I was laughing.'

'Are you sure? It didn't sound like it.'

'And perhaps it would interest you to know what made me laugh. "Why don't you?" you say in that airy way, as if selling Mellingham was a thing that could be done over the counter. Who wants a house nowadays that's miles from anywhere and about the size of Buckingham Palace? And look at the way it eats up money. Repairs, repairs, everlasting repairs—the roof, the stairs, the ceilings, the plumbing, there's no end to it. And that's just inside. Outside, trees needing pruning, hedges needing clipping, acres of grass that doesn't cut itself, and the lake smelling to heaven if the weeds aren't cleaned out every second Thursday. And the tenants. Those farmers sit up at nights trying to think of new ways for you to spend money on them. It's enough to drive a man dotty. I remember, when I was a boy, Father used to take me round the park at Mellingham and say "Some day, Crispin, all this will be yours." He ought to have added, "And may the Lord have mercy on your soul." Bill, can you lend me two hundred and three pounds, six shillings and fourpence?'

Something had told the experienced Willoughby that this jeremiad was going to culminate in some such query, and he exhibited no great concern. He was accustomed to meeting people eager to share his wealth. The exactness of the figures stirred his curiosity a little. Most of those anxious to become his debtors were not so precise.

'Odd sum,' he said.

'It's for the repairs people.'

'Won't they wait?'

'They've been waiting two years.'

'Then they ought to have got the knack of it by now.'

'Don't joke, Bill. It's all very well to make a joke of it, but it's deadly serious. They've sent a man down. He's at the house now.'

'You mean you've got the brokers in?'

'Yes, it's a terrible situation. I live in hourly fear of my paying guests finding out.'

'Give them a good laugh, I should think.'

'They would all leave.'

'Nonsense.'

'It isn't nonsense, they would. So if you won't let me have that money—'

'Of course I'll let you have it. What did you think I was going to do? Though I still feel it's funny, you having a broker's man on the premises, and it's a shame to let him go.'

Crispin gave a short quick gulp like a bulldog trying to swallow a chop whose dimensions it has underestimated. It was plain that a great weight had been lifted from his stooping shoulders, but mingled with the joy, relief and ecstasy that surges over him a borrower of money cannot help experiencing a certain sensation of flatness when his request is granted as soon as uttered. Arab traders in eastern bazaars get this feeling when an impatient customer refuses to haggle. Crispin had anticipated a lengthy session of argument and pleading, and for an instant his emotions were those of one who, descending a staircase in the dark, treads on the last step when it is not there.

Then joy, relief and ecstacy prevailed, and he expressed them with a glad cry.

'That's wonderful of you, Bill. You've saved my life.'

'A mere sample of the way I've been behaving since yesterday afternoon. Did you ever read Oliver Twist?'

'I suppose so, as a kid.'

'Remember the Cheeryble brothers?'

'Vaguely. Sort of elderly boy scouts, weren't they?'

'Exactly, and after yesterday afternoon I'm both of them rolled into one.'

'What happened yesterday afternoon?'

'Look at this.'

Crispin eyed the small object without enthusiasm. It was the miniature of a thin girl in the costume of a past age, and thin girls had never had a great appeal for him. He had always preferred the more opulent type. Both the breach of promise actions of his youth had been brought against him by plaintiffs in the light-heavyweight division. It was difficult to find anything to say, so he merely made a sound as if he were starting to gargle, and Willoughby continued.

'Our great-great grandmother.'

'Oh?'

'Unless it's great-great-great or even more greats than that. I'm never any good at working these things out. When was Gainsborough?'

'In the Regency, wasn't he?'

'I believe so. This is by him. It's called The Girl in Blue. Our great-great grandmother and her sister were twins, and he did miniatures of them both one in blue, the other in green. I've had the other one for years and have been scouring the country for this one. It came up at Sotheby's yesterday. I had to outbid a lot of dealers who spotted how much I wanted it and ran the price up, but I did the stinkers down in the end and got it.'

Crispin found it difficult to repress a sigh. Reason told him that anyone as rich as Bill had a perfect right to collect objects that took his fancy, even if they were nothing much to look at and he had to outbid a lot of stinkers who were running the price up, but it gave him a pang to think of money that might have come in his direction being frittered away on miniatures of great-great-great grandmothers.

'But I mustn't bore you with my petty triumphs,' said Willoughby. 'I'll write that cheque.'

'It's awfully good of you, Bill.'

'Just routine with us Cheerybles. Here you are.'

Crispin took the precious slip of paper, fondled it for a moment like a mother crooning over her first-born, and put it away in the pocket nearest his heart. As he did so, the door in the wall, communicating, he presumed, with Ashby's office or that of Pemberton, opened and a head came through.

'Could you spare a minute, Bill?' said the head.

'That Delahay business?'

'Yes. A couple of points I'd like to take up with you.'

'The way I'm feeling today,' said Willoughby, 'I don't mind if you take up three points, or even four. I'll be back in a second, Crips.'

Chapter Four

Much though Crispin always enjoyed the company of his brother Willoughby, this sudden deprivation of it did nothing to diminish the glow of happiness which their most recent get-together had sent coursing through him. He was not familiar with the works of the poet Browning, but had he been he would have found himself in cordial agreement with the statement of his Pippa in her well-known song that God was in His heaven and all right with the world. Puts the thing in a nutshell, he would have said. He did happen to know that bit in the Psalms about Joy coming in the morning, and he would have contested hotly any suggestion that it didn't. He was, in a word, in excellent shape, in fact, sitting pretty with his hat on the side of his head.

This uplifted mood, it should be noted, was in the deepest sense a triumph of mind over matter, for he had come to London with a stiff neck, the result of sitting in one of the draughts with which the home of his ancestors was so well supplied. It had been a source of considerable anguish on the train, but now he found that if he held his head quite motionless and kept thinking of the cheque that crackled in his pocket, the pain was practically non-existent.

Abandoned by Willoughby, he did what most people do when left alone in strange rooms. Always remembering to keep the head rigid, he wandered to and fro, peering at this, sniffing at that, fingering papers and wondering how that dictaphone thing on the desk worked; and he had just concluded a cursory examination of the shelf of law books and was thinking that he would not care to have to read them himself, when the door leading into the waiting-room burst open and something solid entered at a high rate of speed.

'Sorry, Bill,' said this something, 'Tripped.'

With a sharp cry Crispin put a hand to his neck, which had exploded like a bomb, for under the impact of this abrupt intrusion there had been no question of keeping the head motionless. He stood rubbing it vigorously, but was not so preoccupied with the massage as to be unable to take in the general aspect of the newcomer.

It was a woman who had joined him, and it did not need a second glance to tell him that she was a large woman. Somebody less deeply engaged in trying to soothe his neck might have observed in addition that she was a cheerful woman, a friendly woman and a woman whom it would be a pleasure to know, but these aspects of her did not dawn on him till later.

She was the first to speak. She was one of those women who are always the first to speak.

'Hullo,' she said. 'You aren't Bill Scrope.'

Crispin, courteously stopping rubbing his neck, explained that Bill Scrope had had to step out, to confer, he imagined, with one of his partners, and would be returning shortly.

'I am his brother,' he said, 'his elder brother from the country.'

She uttered a cry that loosened the plaster on the ceiling. 'Are you the fellow who owns this Mellingham Hall joint?'

'I do own Mellingham Hall.'

'I'm coming there tomorrow. I'm Mrs. Clayborne. Well, this is swell, running into you like this. Gives us a chance to get acquainted. Now I shan't feel like a kid going to a new school when I clock in.'

Crispin was frankly appalled. Although this woman

had not spoken a word calculated to bring the blush of shame to the cheek of modesty, she had shocked him to the core. He had told Willoughby of his distaste for hearty women, and here was one, earmarked to share his home, so hearty that the senses reeled. At the thought of her galumphing about Mellingham Hall his head quivered on its base and his neck seemed to be on fire. And when she continued, 'Tell me about this place of yours,' only his breeding enabled him to preserve his customary courtliness.

'Bill,' she proceeded, 'says it dates back to Ethelbert the Unready or someone like that. He says it's all drawbridges and battlements and things, and there's a lake. It must be heavenly.'

Heavenly was not the adjective that came uppermost in Crispin's mind when he thought of Mellingham Hall. It was one he was particularly slow to apply to the lake, an ornate sheet of water which called for the services of two men at exhorbitant salaries if it was to be kept from smelling to heaven. He disliked the lake intensely. Sometimes of an evening when all was still and the rays of the setting sun turned its surface to molten gold, he would stand gazing at it, wondering if anything could be done about the beastly thing. If seven maids with seven mops swept it for half a year, do you suppose, he would ask himself wistfully that they could get it clear? Very improbable, he felt, and who can afford seven ma'ds these days?

Mrs. Clayborne was enlarging on her theme. If she had been a house agent hoping to sell the place to a wavering client, she could not have been more enthusiastic. She said she had read a lot about these old English country homes in novels and all that, but had never come across one yet. Some of her friends on Long Island and at Newport owned pretty palatial joints, but it wasn't the same, they lacked the old-world touch.

'Take you, I mean. I suppose there were Scropes at

35

Mellingham at the time of the Flood.'

It was an unfortunate phrase for her to have chosen, for it reminded Crispin of the night when the rain had come in through the roof, adding a further forty-seven pounds five and ninepence to the bill of the repairs people, who at that point were already more than a hundred and fifty ahead of the game. His hand flew up to his neck, and she looked at him enquiringly.

'Why are you doing that?'

'I beg your pardon?'

'You keep rubbing your neck.'

'I think I must have been sitting in a draught. It is rather painful.'

All the motherliness in Bernadette Clayborne came to the surface as if somebody had pressed a button. It is not only when the brow is racked by pain and anguish that women become ministering angels. They react to stiff necks with equal promptitude.

'We must look into that,' she said. 'Take a chair and lean forward as if you were an early Scrope about to be beheaded on Tower Hill.'

It would be deceiving the wide public for which the chronicler hopes he is writing to say that Crispin enjoyed the next few minutes. They were, indeed, some of the most agonizing he could remember ever living through. He seemed to have delivered himself into the steely clutch of some sort of machine. Only the knowledge that it was firmly fastened on at the roots kept him from being convinced that his head was about to part from the parent spine. He blamed himself for having been so foolish as to sponsor such a performance.

But, as has been well said (by John Dryden, 1631-1700, to keep the record straight), sweet is pleasure after pain. The relief Crispin felt when with a muttered, 'That ought to do it' his assailant relaxed her grip more than compensated for all he had gone through. Shortly before embarking on her activities she had assured him

36

that she would teach his little old neck to take a joke, and her prediction had been amply fulfilled. He sat up. He felt wonderful. He regarded her with gratitude and awe, marvelling that he could ever have thought her unsuitable for residence at Mellingham Hall. It was precisely women of her type that Mellingham Hall had been standing in need of for years.

'I can't thank you enough,' he said fervently. 'The pain has completely gone.'

'I knew it would. I used to do that to my late husband when he had a hangover, which was almost daily, and he said there was nothing like it. And now tell me more about the old home.'

Crispin would have been delighted to do so, but he had just looked at his watch and it had told him that he had no time for idle dalliance. Her conversation enthralled him, but the claims of a to-be-caught train are paramount.

'I wish I could,' he said, 'but I am afraid I must be going, or I shall miss my train.'

'Oh well, I shall be seeing the joint tomorrow.'

'Yes, and I hope you will be very happy there.'

'You bet. And talking of betting, if you have a moment to spare before you go, can you direct me to a good bookie? I've had a hot tip on a horse, and I don't know who to go to over here. Ever hear of a place called Newmarket?'

Crispin was conscious of a nostalgic pang. The name brought back memories of his youth. He had probably lost more money at Newmarket than anywhere.

'That's where it's running a few days from now. So who do I do business with?'

'I used to have an account with Slingsby's. I still have, I imagine.'

'Don't you do any betting nowadays?'

'Never. I have given it up completely.'

'I guess you're wise. I don't often have anything on

myself, but the fellow I was talking to said Brotherly Love would win going away.'

'Brotherly Love?'

'That's its name. What's yours, by the way, apart from the Scrope end?'

'Crispin.'

'For heaven's sake! Not that I'm one to cast the first stone. They christened me Bernadette. Fortunately everyone calls me Barney. You must, too.'

'I will indeed.'

'Can you imagine anyone calling anyone Bernadette? Or Crispin for that matter, or even Willoughby. Nice fellow, Bill. My brother and I are his house guests.'

'So he told me.'

'A bit overweight, isn't he?'

'A little, perhaps.'

'My late husband got that way.'

'Indeed?'

'Couldn't keep him off the starchy foods. But didn't you say you had a train to catch?'

When Willoughby returned from his conference, expecting to see an elder brother, he was momentarily taken aback at finding a changeling in his office.

'Why, hullo, Barney,' he said. 'Where did you come from?'

'Out of the everywhere into here, Bill. I've just had a pleasant visit with Crispin. What a name! I think I'll call him Crippen.'

'What became of him?'

'He had to make a train.'

'Of course, yes, he told me. And what brings you here?'

'I came to borrow a dollar or two. I'm cleaned out.'

'Shopping?'

'And contributing to the support of London's hard-up citizens. There's something about me that seemed to draw the panhandlers the way catnip attracts cats, and I'm down to my last dime. If you don't give me of your plenty, I'll have to skip lunch. Good for the figure, of course, but not a pleasant prospect.'

'My dear Barney, of course you'll lunch with me.'

'The needy never turned from your door, eh?'

'You won't mind my nephew being there?'

'I won't mind a horror from outer space being there if there's lots to eat and drink.'

'There will be. This is a celebration. I've just bought The Girl In Blue.'

'Who's she?'

'She is a miniature by Gainsborough. She is wearing a blue dress, so the late Gainsborough, hunting around for a title, called her The Girl In Blue.'

'Very clever of him. Think like lightning, these artists. Where are we lunching? Excuse me bringing the subject up, but I'm starving.'

'The Savoy.'

'Shall we be going before I swoon?'

'I'm ready. Off to lunch, Mabel,' said Willoughby as they passed through the waiting-room.

'Bon appetit, Mr. Scrope.'

'Good God! French and everything.'

'And if anybody wants him,' said Barney, 'say he's tied up in an orgy and it's no use them waiting, as he doesn't expect to sober up for months and months and months. It's a celebration. He's just been buying girls in blue.'

Chapter Five

The celebration banquet was all that Willoughby had
promised it would be. It ended at about half-past three.
Willoughby went back to his office, Jerry to his rooms,
and Barney resumed her exploration of London. Her
brother Homer at the moment was talking to Vera
Upshaw outside Flannery and Martin's book shop in
Sloane Square, where they had just met.

There was nothing coincidental in their meeting.
One sees in it something of the inevitability which was
such a feature of Greek tragedy. Sloane Square is not
far from Chelsea Square, and any guest of Willoughby's
at 31 Chelsea Square would naturally go to Flannery
and Martin when he wanted a book. Homer, who had
read and admired Vera's *Morning's At Seven*, was
anxious to obtain its successor, the recently published
Daffodil Days. And as for Vera, the flat she shared with
her mother was just around the corner and she looked
in on Flannery and Martin a good deal to see if they had
any copies of her brain child. Sometimes she came in
the morning, sometimes in the evening. Today she had
come in the afternoon, and she was still there when
Homer reached journey's end.

The gentlemanly young clerk who presided over the
shop would gladly have seen her leave. Charmed at the
outset of their relations by her radiant beauty, he had
come to dread her visits. It seemed impossible, when
she commented on the absence of copies of *Daffodil
Days*, to convince her that he was just a Hey-you about

the place and was not invited to join the discussion when Flannery and his partner Martin were deciding what books to stock. Mere quibbling his reasoning struck her as, and she mentioned this to him.

The clerk was mopping his forehead, wondering what could have induced him to sign on for his current post when there was such a brisk demand for strong young men to clean streets, and Vera had turned to run her eye over the shelf where belles lettres of an older vintage were kept, to make sure that *Daffodil Days* had not slipped in there by mistake, when the door leading into the street opened, admitting a rush of warm air and something short, stout and American which seemed at first sight to be all horn-rimmed spectacles. She gave it no attention beyond a quick uninterested glance. Short stout Americans meant nothing to her, whether spectacled or with 20-20 vision. Only when, addressing the clerk, he uttered the astounding words 'Have you a book called *Daffodil Days* by Vera Upshaw?' did she whip round, her lips parted, her eyes wide, and her lovely body tingling as if some practical joker had run a powerful instalment of electricity through it. It is doubtful if a girl had been so thrilled since the one in the Indian Mutiny who heard the skirl of the bagpipes at the siege of Cawnpore.

Nor was the clerk unmoved. A suspicion was beginning to steal over him that his employers had passed up a good thing. Vera's enthusiasm he could overlook as pure routine, but unless the man behind the spectacles was her uncle or father or something, this sudden call for copies of *Daffodil Days* might well be the start of a big popular demand; the first scattered raindrops, as it were, that herald the deluge. If, that is to say, one short stout person wanted to read *Daffodil Days*, it showed that it could be done, and who was to say that others would not want to do it.

He was shaken, but he tried to recover his poise.

Regretfully confessing that the book was not at the moment in stock, he suggested to Homer that he should get it for him, an offer which Homer declined, saying that he would be leaving England on the following day. The clerk then put forward as possible substitutes *My Life On The Links* by Sandy McHoots (as told to Colin Jeffson) and *Theatre Memories* by Dame Flora Faye (as told to Reginald Tressilian), but no business resulted, and Homer was on the pavement outside the shop and about to head for Chelsea Square, when a voice said: 'Excuse me', and he turned and, having turned, stood rigid, like someone in a fairy story on whom a spell has been cast.

Homer's life had been singularly free from beautiful girls. He did not go out in the evening very much, almost never to parties where such fauna abound, and during office hours a corporation lawyer's chances of seeing anything in the Helen of Troy class are limited. The impact of Vera Upshaw was in consequence extremely powerful. He gaped at her like a spectacled goldfish, and it was she who opened the conversation. Her manner was brisk and free from diffidence. If a criticism must be made, it was, if anything, perhaps too firm and authoritative. Her public was not so large that she intended to let a potential reader get away.

'I think I heard you asking for *Daffodil Days*,' she said crisply.

Homer's vocal cords were not in the best of shape, but he was able to reply huskily that this was so, adding that they hadn't got it.

'I know they hadn't,' said Vera with bitterness. 'That's the slipshod way book shops are run over here. Is it the same in America?'

A little surprised at her penetration in guessing his nationality, Homer replied that he had always found the New York book shops pretty good. He was, however, scarcely to be regarded as a normal customer, for he seldom read anything but legal tomes.

'I am a corporation lawyer. My literature is mostly technical.'

'Have you been in England long?'

'A few days only. It is not, of course, my first visit. I have always been fond of London.'

'Though I suppose your wife prefers Paris? Most American women do.'

'I am not married.'

'Oh. Well, what I was going to say was that I shall be very glad to give you a copy of *Daffodil Days*.'

'No, no, really, I couldn't think—'

'I have several. I wrote it.'

Homer's eyes widened to about the size of standard golf balls. He gasped a startled 'Really?'

'It is my second book. I had another out last year called—'

'*Morning's At Seven*,' said Homer devoutly.

'Don't tell me you read it.'

'I read it several times.'

'But it wasn't published in America.'

'An English friend sent it to me.'

'And you really liked it?'

'I thought it admirable.'

'How very gratifying. And how strange.'

'I beg your pardon?'

'You said you only read law books.'

'Except when I find a *Morning's At Seven*,' said Homer, coming within an ace of adding 'Dear lady'. 'I make an exception in the case of charming, delightful, dainty works that make me feel as if I were sitting beside a rippling brook, listening to its silver music. It had what so few books have nowadays, charm.'

Well put, thought Homer, and Vera thought so, too. There had been a few reviews of *Morning's At Seven*, but only in obscure provincial papers and only things like 'will help to pass an idle hour' and 'not unreadable'.

This was the real stuff.

'You speak like a poet,' she said, feeling for the first time that the aura of wealth that floated about him like some lovely scent was not his only claim to her esteem, and she bestowed on him one of those melting glances which hit a susceptible man like the kick of a mule.

'In a small way I am,' said Homer, framing the words with difficulty, for the effects of that look still lingered. 'I write little verses in my spare time.'

'Have they been published?'

'Very occasionally.'

'You must make a book of them.'

'I don't think I could quite aspire to that.'

'Nonsense. You're much too modest. And now I must ask who and where.'

'I beg your pardon?'

'What name and what address. Who do I send the book to?'

'Homer Pyle is the name, but—'

'Of course. I remember. You said you were leaving England tomorrow.'

'Yes, I am going to Brussels for the P.E.N. conference.'

'Why, so am I.'

Once more Homer found it difficult to speak, and when he did, all he could manage was a weak 'Really?'

'So we shall be seeing something of each other. And about the book. I can give it to you now, if you will come round to where I live. It's only a step, and I should like you to meet my mother. Her name will probably be familiar to you. Dame Flora Faye.'

2

A girl who has brought a strange man home to meet her mother, rather in the tentative spirit of a dog bringing a bone into a drawing-room, naturally seeks the earliest opportunity of learning the latter's opinion of him. Vera, having seen Homer out at the end of his visit, returned to where Dame Flora Faye reclined in her arm chair, and Dame Flora looked up at her from its depths with an enquiring, 'Well?'

'Just what I was going to say to you,' said Vera.

'Meaning what did I think of Mr. Pyle?'

'Exactly.'

'Well, I'll tell you, my poppet.'

Surprisingly in a woman who in the course of a long career had spread more nervous breakdowns among directors, leading men, supporting players and assistant stage managers than any other female star of her weight and age, Dame Flora's vocal delivery was soft and gentle. She had never been one of those empresses of stormy emotion so popular at one time on the silent screen who raged and bellowed; she got her effects more subtly. One of her playwrights, speaking from the nursing home where he was recovering from mental exhaustion, had once described her as the vulture who cooed like a dove.

'It depends,' she continued, 'on what aspect of him you have in mind. If you refer to his looks, I doubt if he will ever win a beauty contest, even a seaside one. On the other hand, he is an American corporation lawyer, and one of the first lessons we learn in life is that there is no such thing as an American corporation lawyer who does not wear hundred-dollar bills next his skin summer and winter. I should imagine that when Mr. Pyle is called upon to act for a company in its suit against another company, his clients consider themselves lucky if they come out of it after paying his fee with enough to buy a frugal lunch next day. Give me another cup of tea, dearie, and pass me those little cakes with pink sugar on top.'

'They're fattening.'

'Everything in life that's any fun, as somebody wisely

observed, is either immoral, illegal or fattening. Returning to your question, I think I know why you asked it. You did not fail to notice that you had made a marked impression on this hand across the sea. He couldn't take his eyes off you, and I'm not surprised, because you're the most beautiful thing on earth, my lamb. So you're saying to yourself "Where do I go from here?", and you naturally come to mother for advice. I could give it to you better if I knew how matters are between you and this ginger-headed pavement artist you've got engaged to. As I understand it, he has money coming to him, but it's in trust and his trustee won't give it up and you very prudently refuse to marry him till the deadlock melts, if that's what deadlocks do. I may be thinking of ice packs. You're in the position of a manager who has a show that's a turkey at the box office, and he thinks "Shall I put up the fortnight's notice or shall I carry on on the chance of business improving?" If he knows what's good for him, he puts up the notice, and I advise you to do the same, my dream child.'

'It isn't quite like that, mother. Gerald is getting his money today.'

'How do you know?'

'I told him what to do. I've been studying up the legal end of the thing. It's too long to explain, but it all turns on the trust being terminable. It is terminable, so Mr. Scrope won't have a leg to stand on. Gerald was lunching with him today, so by now everything must be settled.'

'I see. But even so, what on earth do you want with him when you can have this excellent corporation lawyer with about a hundred times as much? I wouldn't call Mrs. Homer Pyle a euphonious name, but I strongly urge you to take it on. I'm not asking you to love him, mind you. I nearly married for love when I was young and foolish, but I came out of the ether in time and saw there was nothing in it. Mutual respect is what matters in marriage. Pyle respects you, doesn't he? Of course he does. And don't tell me you don't respect someone who makes his sort of money. And you'll be together in Brussels for I don't know how long. And you get lovelier every day. And a man who writes little poems can't have any sales resistance. Why, the thing's in the bag. The scenario couldn't read better if it had been turned out in Hollywood with six supervisors and fifteen writers working on it. Don't wait, honeychile. Get on the phone and tell your French polisher it's all off. I never could see what you saw in him in the first place.'

No daughter could have failed to be stirred by such admirable counsel coming from mother who knew best, and Vera was plainly swayed. Nevertheless, she was dubious.

'But how can I? I wouldn't know what to say.'

Dame Flora smiled a gentle smile. Rising from her chair, she put an arm round her little girl and gave her a kiss, as she had done to a dozen daughters in a dozen productions since the march of time had forced her to play mothers.

'Don't worry your pretty head about that, my pet. I'll do the ringing up. You say that you would be at a loss for words. I won't. Words are the last thing I'm ever at a loss for. I know exactly how the scene should go. I tell him you think he's weak, and you must have a strong man for a husband, because you need someone to guide you and make decisions for you. So-and-so I'll say and so-and-so and so-and-so, and I'll wind up by telling him you will always look on him as a dear, dear friend and will follow his career with considerable interest. Any questions?'

'Oh, mother!' said Vera.

The policeman on the corner, watching Homer start on his journey back to Chelsea Square, probably debated with himself the advisability of weaving a circle round him thrice, his aspect being so plainly that of one who on honeydew had fed and drunk the milk of Paradise. Only the fact of his wearing spectacles and having a hat on kept attention from being drawn to his flashing eyes and floating hair. He was, indeed, in as uplifted a mood as if he had just received a six-figure fee for negotiating a merger between a multi-million corporation and another multi-million corporation.

His visit to the home of Dame Flora Faye and her daughter Vera had been the most triumphant success. He had expected to pop in and pop out again in a matter of minutes, and they had kept him there for nearly two hours, and it had been delightful, perfectly delightful.

He had found Dame Flora charming. Too often artists of her eminence are inclined to be cold and distant towards those as alien to their rarefied atmosphere as corporation lawyers, but she, on being informed that that was his walk in life, could not have been more cordial. She had shown the greatest interest in his prosaic profession. He could well understand why for so many theatrical seasons worshipping audiences had been falling at her feet and why a gracious sovereign, feeling that there is nothing like a dame, had made her one.

As for her daughter Vera, she had been a revelation to him. His first act on reaching his destination was to sit down and write a poem directly inspired by her.

Barney came in as he was finishing it, and he greeted her in the precise and formal manner in which he always greeted her.

'Ah, Bernadette.'

'Hi, Homer.'

'Did you have a pleasant afternoon?'

'Fine.'

'Where did you go?'

'Hither and thither, seeing the sights. I did a little shopping.'

Homer started violently, dislodging the fountain pen which had been assisting him to put his soul on paper.

'You didn't—?'

She smiled the indulgent smile she usually reserved for the foolish babblings of doctors who told her she smoked too much.

'No, no, all cash transactions. You were quite wrong about that business at Guildenstern's. I keep telling you it was purely experimental. For some reason I found myself thinking of Aunt Betsy, and I said to myself If she could pinch things from under the noses of department store detectives, I ought to be able to do it, too, so I gave it a try. It was a mistake, of course, I can see that now. It might have been better not to have made the experiment. But how was I to know that these fellows have eyes at the back of their heads?'

The explanation she offered was the same which Homer had put before Duane Stottlemeyer at the start of their interview, but he had not believed it then and he did not believe it now. He was convinced that his sister, like the Aunt Betsy she had mentioned, had some defect in her mental and spiritual make-up which caused anything that was not nailed down to have an irresistible attraction for her. His gratitude to Duane for that admirable suggestion of his increased daily, and he hoped his next song of protest would find a sympathetic editor and one with more of the Santa Claus spirit, when it came to payment, than most of the editors of his experience. Thanks to Duane, Bernadette would be safely at Mellingham Hall tomorrow, far away from the insidious temptations of department stores.

Barney, having made clear her motives for trying to get things on the cheap at Guildenstern's, changed the subject. It was not one that interested her greatly.

'By the way,' she said, 'I met Bill Scrope's brother Crispin this morning, the one who owns Mellingham Hall.'

'Indeed? Where did you meet him?'

'At Bill's office. I'd looked in to give him a miniature I'd picked up for a few shillings at a hock shop, knowing that he collected the darned things, and the first thing he did was show me one he'd just bought for some colossal sum. By Gainsborough, I think he said it was, one of the guys up top, anyway. So naturally I didn't mention my five-shilling exhibit. It would have been like entering a mongrel at the Westminster Kennel Show.'

'And how did you get on with Mr. Crispin Scrope?'

'Swell. We're practically kissing cousins.'

'Good. Good. Then you are sure to be happy at Mellingham Hall,' said Homer, relieved.

His relief lasted till the dinner hour, when it became replaced by a growing uneasiness. This was caused by his sister Bernadette's outspoken enthusiasm for the Gainsborough miniature of which she had spoken.

Exhibited at the table by Willoughby with a collector's pardonable pride, it drew from her a stream of what are called marked tributes. Gainsborough, if he had heard them, would have felt that though he had always known he was good, he had never supposed he was as good as all that. She called it cute. She thought the little girl too ducky for words, though needing a square meal or two to fatten her up. She reached for it to examine it more closely, and it seemed to Homer that there was a glitter in her eyes which he did not like at all. Just so, he told himself, they must have glittered as she went her way through Guildenstern's department store, and admirable though the dinner was that Willoughby's cook had served up, it is not too much to say that it turned to ashes in Homer's mouth. He sat crumbling bread and fearing the shape of things to come.

He rose from the table at the conclusion of the meal empty as far as proteins and carbohydrates were concerned, but full of a stern resolve. He did not like what he had to do, but he knew that it was his obvious duty to do it. Briskly though his flesh crawled at the prospect, Willoughby must be warned.

The opportunity of warning him came when Barney had gone to bed and he and his host were having a last drink in the study, which in this bachelor establishment was the hub and centre of things. Willoughby, preparing to retire, had risen and placed the miniature on the mantelpiece, giving Homer the opening he needed.

'You aren't going to leave it there?' he said, and Willoughby said: 'Where else?'

'I would have thought you would have locked it up, a valuable object like that.'

The suggestion amused Willoughby.

'Think somebody's going to pinch it?'

'I should be apprehensive if it were mine.'

'There are burglar alarms on all the windows.'

'But is that enough?' said Homer, shrinking like a salted snail at the thought of having to reveal the skeleton in the family cupboard, but feeling that if the revelation must be made, this was the moment for a conscientious man to make it. 'Has it ever occurred to you, Scrope, to wonder why I have been so anxious to find some remote spot for my sister to go to? You can imagine how distressing it is for me to say this, but it is my duty to tell you that it is not safe to leave her within reach of anything valuable.'

He had expected his statement to be badly received, and he had not erred. Willoughby stiffened formidably.

The suspicion that this was a joke of some kind he had dismissed without hesitation. Corporation lawyers do not drink too much at dinner and indulge in tasteless humour afterwards. It was plain that his guest meant what he had said, and there was frostiness in the gaze he directed at him.

'Are you suggesting that your sister is a thief?'

'I am afraid that it is more than a suggestion. Just before we sailed she was arrested for shoplifting at one of the large department stores, and there was no question of anything in the nature of a mistake; her pockets were full of costume jewellery. Fortunately the manager of the store was a man I had known at college, and he consented not to prefer charges. But he made it a condition that Bernadette leave America at once, and a friend of mine advised me to place her as a paying guest in an English country house, where she would be out of the reach of temptation.'

The minute or so this longish speech had taken to deliver had given Willoughby time to recover from his shock and marshal his thoughts. He was able now to put his finger on the flaw in Homer's reasoning.

'I can see how unpleasant it must have been for you,' he said, his genial self again and the coldness gone from his voice, 'but I don't feel that you need be disturbed. She must have done it as a joke, to see if she could get away with it.'

'I thought that at first, but I have changed my mind.'

'Then she probably felt that it was no worse than smuggling stuff through the Customs. In any case, you can't tell me that a woman like Barney, whatever she might do in a department store, would abuse a friend's hospitality by sneaking things from his house while she was a guest there. I would trust her if I had the crown jewels here.'

'Then you won't lock it up?'

'Of course I won't. I should feel I was insulting her.'

'She wouldn't know.'

'*I* should know, and I shouldn't be able to look myself in the face when I shaved. I'd have to grow a beard. Let's drop the subject and go to bed. I have to be at the office early tomorrow. I'm going off for a short holiday, and there are all sorts of things to clean up before I leave.'

Homer went to bed, but not to sleep. He had slid between the sheets a few minutes before midnight. At one a.m. he was still restless and wakeful. Nor had conditions improved by two. At two-fifteen his mind was made up. He rose, put on a dressing-gown, crept down to the study, took the miniature from the mantelpiece, deposited it in the middle drawer of the desk, closed the drawer and went back to his bed. Tomorrow afternoon, if he could not manage it earlier, he would telephone Willoughby and put him abreast.

He was asleep by two-forty-seven.

Chapter Six

Jerry, too, had passed a disturbed night. Quite a few of the hours that should have been reserved for slumber had been taken over by meditation.

The problem he was hoping to solve was one which keeps cropping up in the Advice To The Lovelorn columns. What he was anxious to figure out was What should a young man do who, betrothed to Girl A, unexpectedly finds himself in love with Girl B, the latter plainly the mate intended for him from the beginning of time by the authorities who arrange these things.

Had he been in America, he could have consulted Dear Abby or Doctor Joyce Brothers. In London he could think of no-one on whose acumen he could place a similar reliance. There was Aunt Phyllis on the weekly paper for which he did a good deal of work, but Aunt Phyllis was a fat man in his fifties with a passion for lager beer and a ribald outlook on life, and he shrank from confiding in him.

Sitting down after breakfast and lighting the after-breakfast pipe, he set himself to review the situation.

It was beyond a doubt not the most agreeable of situations to be in, but in one respect he could see that he had something to be thankful for. He had promised Vera that at that Savoy lunch he would take up once again with his uncle Bill the matter of his money, this time being very firm and resolute, and but for the addition of Barney to the guest list he would presumably have done so. And had he done so, there was no question

54

what would have happened. Uncle Bill had been in the sort of effervescent high spirits which make a man leap at the opportunity of doing anything to oblige anybody. Asked for the money, he would have had his cheque book and fountain pen out of his pocket with the swiftness of a conjurer de-rabbiting a top hat, and the last obstacle to union with Vera, only daughter of the late Charles Upshaw and his wife Dame Flora Faye, would have been removed. The squeak had been so narrow that, warm though the morning was, a chill passed through Jerry from top hair to bedroom slippers as he thought of it.

But his guardian angel had seen to it that Barney should be there, and he was suitably grateful to him. He wished he could find him and slap him on the back and tell him how deeply he appreciated his work. Not a hope, of course. Guardian angels keep themselves to themselves and are hard to get hold of when you want them.

Well, he reflected as he lit his second pipe, so far so good, but he was a clear-thinking young man and he did not try to disguise it from himself that he was still separated from the happy ending by a wide margin. His guardian angel had certainly given satisfaction to date, but there remained much for him to do, and there must be no folding of the hands, no sitting back and taking it easy, no slackening of the will to win on his part. He must continue on his toes as sedulously as ever until that unfortunate betrothal was a thing of the past. For from whatever angle you looked at the set-up and however much you refused to face facts, there was no getting away from it that he was still engaged to Vera Upshaw and unless prompt steps were taken through the proper channels would ere long be walking up the aisle with her in a morning coat and spongebag trousers, which, she would probably hiss in his car in that critical way of hers, needed pressing.

He had been giving the peril that encompassed him the tensest thought for a considerable time, when a glance at the morning paper which lay on the table beside him reminded him that today was Wednesday and, arising from that, that life is stern and life is earnest. Reluctantly, for he would have preferred to brood indefinitely, he rose, shaved, took a shower bath and put on shirt, tie, flannel suit and shoes. This done, he went out, carrying his portfolio.

Wednesday is the day when cartoonists pack up their week's cartoons and take them round the magazines for the inspection of art editors. A dozen or so nervous cartoonists would assemble outside the art editor's door and be called in one by one by a bodiless head which came poking out at intervals, as a rule smoking an evil-smelling cigar. The atmosphere created was much the same as that which prevails in a dentist's waiting-room.

Generally, on Wednesdays Jerry had to sit in several waiting-rooms before making a sale, for art editors, like Queen Victoria, are not easily amused, but today it was as if Fate, sympathizing with the difficulties which were casting a shadow over his love life, had very decently decided to do something to cheer him up. Feeling that there he would at least get a friendly reception, he had started his quest at the offices of the weekly paper which took so much of his work, the one for which Aunt Phyllis conducted the Advice To The Lovelorn column, and the benevolent occupant of the editorial chair made history by accepting not one whimsical cartoon but the entire contents of his portfolio, seeming disappointed that these were all he had to offer.

It was a unique happening, and its effect on him was to induce in him emotions similar to those which had so stirred his Uncle Willoughby when The Girl In Blue had come into his possession. It seemed to him, as it had seemed to Willoughby, that a triumph like this must be celebrated by a lunch that would go down in legend and song. It remained only to select the appropriate restaurant, and after some thought he decided on the grill-room at Barribault's world-famous hostelry. Anything less luxurious would be an anti-climax.

As he entered that stamping ground of Texas millionaires and Indian Maharajahs, one thing alone prevented his feeling of what the French call *bien être* being perfect. It was the fact that he *was* alone. All around him were rich men and fair women digging in and getting theirs in couples, but he had no-one to help him celebrate. How merrily, he felt, he would sail into the bill of fare if the girl he loved were there.

At this moment he saw that she was. She was drinking coffee at a table near the door.

He halted, transfixed. A Texas millionaire, who was following him into the grill room, rammed him in the small of the back, but he scarcely noticed him. He was staring as Homer Pyle had stared when first encountering Vera Upshaw, with this difference that Homer had had no doubt from the start that what he was goggling at was a corporeal entity, while he was under the impression that he was seeing something in the nature of a mirage or figment of the imagination, possibly an astral body that had somehow managed to get transported from Bournemouth to the west end of London. Then she looked up, smiled an enchanting smile and waved a cordial coffee spoon.

'Well!' she said, as he bounded forward, tripping over a Maharajah. 'G. G. F. West, if I mistake not.'

Jerry collapsed on to the banquette beside her. Somebody in the vicinity seemed to be playing the trap drums, but investigation told him that it was only his heart beating.

'This,' he said, 'is amazing. I thought you were in Bournemouth.'

'I am in Bournemouth, or I shall be there again ere yonder sun has set. I came up for the day on business.'

'Oh, you aren't here permanently?' he said, disappointed.

'No, just passing through.'

'That's too bad. Well, let's have lunch.'

'I've had lunch.'

'Have another.'

'No, thanks. But don't let me stop you.'

'It would take a good deal to stop me,' said Jerry. 'If you must know it, I came in here to gorge. And to check the "Greedy pig" which I see trembling on your lips, I must explain that my mid-day meal today was to be a celebration. I don't know how much you know about peddling cartoons?'

'Not much.'

'Well, on Wednesday you make the round of the magazines with your little portfolio, and if you're lucky, you sell a single cartoon after four or five unsuccessful shots, art editors as a class being incapable of recognizing a good thing when they see one.'

'Like the base Indian one used to hear about at school who threw the pearl away richer than all his tribe. Why base?'

'He sang bass!'

'Of course. Well, press on. You were saying that you're lucky if you sell a single cartoon after four or five unsuccessful shots.'

'Six or seven sometimes.'

'But today?'

'Precisely. But today I sold my whole output at the very first place I went to.'

'Why, that's wonderful!'

'It's stupendous'.

'I don't wonder you felt you had to celebrate. I only hope I'll have the same sort of luck.'

'In what way?'

'This business of mine I've come up from Bournemouth about. What would you say it meant when a

58

lawyer writes to you saying that if you call on him, you will learn of something to your advantage?'

'It ought to mean money.'

'I trust it does, because on the strength of those kind words I did myself well at lunch. I felt I could afford it.'

'Then you've had that sort of letter?'

'It came this morning.'

'It ought to mean that someone's left you a legacy.'

'It ought, oughtn't it. But I can't think who.'

'Have any of your relations died lately?'

'Not that I know of. And none of them have any money, anyway.'

'Some old school crony from Cheltenham? Some girl who scored a goal at hockey because you passed to her at just the right moment.'

'But what would she be doing, dying? She would be in her early twenties.'

'I see what you mean. Yes, it's mysterious.'

'My aunt thinks it's a trap.'

'What kind of trap?'

'White slavers. They lure me into their den, pretending to be lawyers, and chloroform me and ship me off to South America.'

'Why you particularly?'

'I suppose they've got to chloroform somebody.'

'Yes, there's that, of course. And they just happened to hit on you.'

'My aunt thinks they keep a list.'

'Would you say it seemed likely?'

'Nothing my aunt thinks ever seems likely.'

'Where did these lawyers write from? Don't you feel that a lot depends on that? I mean, if it was from Joe the Lascar's underground cellar in Limehouse, that doesn't look so good.'

'No, the address is all right. Bedford Row. And the firm sounds respectable. Scrope, Ashby and Pemberton. The one who signed the letter was Willoughby Scrope.'

'Well, I'll be ... damned I suppose is the word I'm groping for.'

'And why, Mr. Bones, will you be damned?'

'Because Willoughby Scrope's my uncle.'

'Really? And you think he's all right?'

'A splendid fellow.'

'Doesn't chloroform girls?'

'Wouldn't dream of it. Wouldn't drug them, either. If he offers you a drink, have no hesitation in downing it.'

'Well, that's fine. You've eased my mind.'

These conversational exchanges, though set down in that way for the sake of convenience, had actually not been continuous. Jerry had abandoned his original idea of making the sort of lunch that would have appealed to the Roman emperor Vitellius, but he had summoned waiters and taken nourishment. Barribault's do not like it if you just go there and sit. He had now finished a modest meal and was lighting a cigarette, having seen to it that his companion was supplied with one.

'Lucky my aunt isn't here,' she said, puffing.

'She doesn't approve of smoking?'

'She thinks it gives you dyspepsia, sleeplessness, headache, weak eyes, asthma, bronchitis, rheumatism, lumbago and sciatica and brings you out in red spots.'

'I would like to meet your aunt. Interesting woman.'

'She wouldn't like to meet you. You're an artist.'

'Ah yes, all those Russian princesses. She strikes me as a bit on the austere side. Why do you go back to her?'

'I must. And that reminds me. That dinner of ours.'

'I'm counting the minutes.'

'Well, I'm afraid you'll have to count a few more, because I'm postponing it.'

'Oh hell, if I may use the expression. Why?'

'I'd forgotten it was her birthday on Friday. Shall we make it Saturday?'

'I suppose so, if we must, but I still say Oh, hell.'

'Barribault's about eight?'

'That's right.'

'Then it's on. And I'm off. If I don't see your uncle at once, I shall miss the only good train in the afternoon. Is this Bedford Row near here?'

'Not very.'

'Then you had better put me into a taximeter cab.'

The cab rolled off. Jerry walked back to his flat. He had to. Barribault's had drawn heavily of his assets, and mere charm of manner is never accepted by taxi drivers as a substitute for cash.

But he would have walked even if he had been in funds, for he wanted to study this problem of his from every angle, and he always thought better when in motion.

It was a problem that needed all the thought he could give it. The recent encounter had deepened his conviction that there was only one girl in the world he could possibly marry, and as of even date he could see no way of avoiding marrying another. An impasse, if ever there was one. King Solomon and Brigham Young would have taken it in their stride, but he could see no solution.

Reaching home, he sat down and continued to ponder. He recalled a musical comedy in which the comedian, reminded by the soubrette that they were engaged to be married, had said, 'I forgot to tell you about that, it's off', and he was thinking wistfully that they managed these things better in musical comedy, when the telephone rang and over the wire came floating the lovely voice of the Dame of the British Empire who, he greatly feared, was about to become his mother-in-law. It surprised him a good deal, for she was not in the habit of chatting with him over the telephone. Indeed, she had always given him the impression that it revolted her to talk to him at all.

'Gerald? Oh, good afternoon, Gerald. I hope I am not interrupting your work?'

'No, I never work on Wednesday.'

'How I envy you. I am resting at the moment, but as a rule the Wednesday matinée is the curse of my life. Did you ever hear the story of the actress who was walking past the fish shop and saw all those fishy eyes staring at her "That reminds me," she said, "I have a Wednesday matinée." But I didn't ring you up to tell you funny stories. My mission is a serious one. I have just been seeing Vera off to Brussels and she gave me a most unpleasant task to perform.'

'Oh, I'm sorry.'

'I'm afraid you will be even sorrier when you hear what it is,' said Dame Flora, cooing like a turtle dove in springtime.

2

Dame Flora was a woman of her word. She had promised her ewe lamb that she would get her betrothed on the telephone and make it clear to him that his idea that wedding bells were going to ring out was a mistaken one, and this she proceeded to do. It was a masterly performance, for which she would have been justified in charging him the price of an orchestra stall.

'I know you will understand, Gerald,' she concluded. 'And Vera wants me to tell you that she will always look on you as a dear, dear friend. Goodbye, Gerald, goodbye, goodbye.'

The receiver shook in Jerry's hand as he replaced it. In the course of her remarks Dame Flora had stressed the fact that the ewe lamb considered him weak, and weak was what he was feeling, if weak is not too weak a word. Boneless is more the one a stylist like Gustave Flaubert would have chosen, though being French he would have used whatever the French is for boneless —*étourdit* perhaps, or something like that.

It was, of course, the bonelessness of relief, yet there again one needs a stronger word. One does not speak of the condemned man on the scaffold who sees a messenger galloping up on a foaming horse with a reprieve in his hand as feeling relieved. Perhaps the best way out of the difficulty is to say that Jerry's emotions at this high spot in his life were very much those of Crispin Scrope as he watched his brother Willoughby write a check for two hundred and three pounds six shillings and fourpence.

For an age he sat stunned, his mind a mere welter of incoherence, conscious only of a reverent awe for the guardian angel who had somehow—he could not imagine how—engineered this astounding coup. Then there crept in the realization that it is not enough merely to contemplate a good thing; to get the best results one must push it along. Free now to woo the girl he loved, he must lose no time in starting to do so. They would be dining together next Saturday, but it would be madness to hang about twiddling his thumbs till then. At times like this every minute counts. Who knew that long before Saturday some dashing young spark at Bournemouth might not have snapped her up? He had never been in Bournemouth, but he presumed they had dashing young sparks there. He must go instantly to Bournemouth and make his presence felt.

And his first move must be to find out her name, a thing he had once again carelessly omitted to do. A wooer who attempts to woo without having this vital fact at his fingers' ends can never hope to make a real success of his courtship.

Fortunately it was simple. She had gone off to see his Uncle Bill and learn of something to her advantage, so all he had to do was pick up the telephone . . .

'Uncle Bill? This is Jerry.'

Willoughby's reception of the information lacked cordiality. He was on the point of leaving for his short golfing holiday, and he had not given himself too much time for his train.

'It would be,' he said churlishly. 'You would come ringing up when I've about five minutes to get to the station.'

'Are you off somewhere?'

'Sandwich. Golfing.'

'Well, I won't keep you a minute. It's a girl. I'm giving her dinner on Saturday.'

'Doesn't your Vera object?'

'No, that's all right. Vera's broken the engagement.'

'I'm delighted to hear it. She's no good to man or beast.'

'And this other girl's wonderful.'

'Then what's your problem?'

'I don't know her name.'

'Didn't you ask her?'

'No.'

'Why not?'

'We got talking of other things and I sort of over-looked it.'

A sigh came over the wire.

'I've been afraid something like this would happen ever since you were dropped on your head as a baby. Goodbye, Jerry.'

'No, no, wait, Uncle Bill, don't hang up. You know this girl. She came to see you this afternoon about a letter you wrote her. You told her that if she got in touch with you, she would learn of something to her advantage.'

A snort at the other end of the wire told Jerry that he had at last succeeded in enchaining his uncle's interest.

'Good Lord! Was that the one? I remember now she said something about having met you. Her name's Hunnicut. Jane Hunnicut. She's an air hostess.'

'I know.'

'But I don't suppose she'll be one much longer. She's come into money.'

'I thought she might.'

'From some old man of the name of Donahue she appears to have met in the course of her air-hostessing. He died the other day. I haven't all the particulars, but I've been on the phone with the New York lawyers, and they tell me he had no near relations, so no chance of the will being contested. The whole pile comes to Jane, and good luck to her. She struck me as a very nice girl, who thoroughly deserves to hit the jackpot. She'll get between one and two million dollars. Goodbye, curse you, I must rush, or I'll miss that blasted train.'

3

Thus Willoughby, and with no further delay he bounded off with his suitcase and his golf clubs.

He left an affectionate nephew staring before him with unseeing eyes, his general aspect that of one who, like Lot's wife, has been unexpectedly turned into a pillar of salt.

Jerry was frankly appalled. To Jane Hunnicut, he presumed, these pennies from heaven, if that was where old Mr. Donahue had gone, had brought happiness and rejoicing, for even in this era of depressed currencies between one and two million dollars is always well worth having, but he saw in her sudden access to the higher income tax brackets the crashing of all his hopes and dreams.

Everyone's squeamishness starts somewhere, and his sprang into life at the thought of becoming that familiar figure of farce, the impecunious suitor who is trying to marry the heiress. For no matter how sincere the love of such a man may be, if he shows a disposition to woo a millionairess, the world sniggers: and anyone who has had a world sniggering at him will testify that the experience is a most disagreeable one.

We pencil Jerry in, then, as a soul in torment and turn to Mabel the receptionist.

Chapter Seven

For the greater part of the day Mabel sat at her desk thinking of absolutely nothing, coming out of her coma only when some caller arrived and it was necessary to ask his name; but towards the end of the afternoon it was as if new life had been breathed into the inert frame. Her thoughts had turned to tea. Today this moment had coincided with Willoughby's dash through the waiting-room and disappearance into the world beyond. As his flying coat tails vanished and all was still again a strong yearning filled her for the evening cuppa.

Usually she sent Percy the office boy out for it, but with her employer absent it seemed an excellent opportunity to refresh herself for once from a china cup instead of one of those cardboard things. She welcomed, too, the chance of doing a little window shopping.

Percy, when not running errands, spent his time in a small cubbyhole down the corridor reading the comics. He could be summoned by a bell, and she went into Willoughby's office to press the requisite button.

'I'm going out, young Perce,' she said when he appeared. 'I shan't be long. Park yourself at my desk and take any telephone calls. Tell anyone who wants Mr. Scrope that he's gone off for a short holiday and would they care to leave a message. And be careful when you answer the phone to say "Office of Scrope, Ashby and Pemberton" and not "Yus?". I've had to speak to you about that before.'

She was gone some twenty minutes. Returning all

tuned up and ready for another spell of sitting and thinking of nothing, she was pleased to see Percy at his post. Full of tea, buns and the milk of human kindness, she might have patted him on the head, had it not been for the peculiarly repellent brand of hair oil which he affected.

'Any calls?' she asked, and Percy replied that there had been only one.

'For Mr. Scrope?'

'Yus.'

'I hope you didn't say "Yus". Who was it?'

'Sounded like Bile. He was drunk.'

'What!'

'You heard. He was as stewed as a prune.'

'Why do you think that?'

'Because of what he said. I wasn't on to him at first. He was all right when he asked for the boss, didn't hiccup or anything. I said the boss had hopped it and would he care to leave a message. Then guess what.'

'What?'

'He said "Yus, tell him I put Minnie Shaw in the middle drawer of the desk".'

'Percy, you're making this up.'

'Honest to God I'm not. That's what he said. I wrote it down.'

'Minnie Shaw?'

'Yus.'

'Put her in the middle drawer of the desk?'

'Yus.'

'How do you put a girl in the middle drawer of a desk? There wouldn't be room.'

'There would if you chopped her up first. But I could see it was just the drunken babble of someone who had been mopping it up all day like a vacuum cleaner, so I dismissed the thing from my mind.'

'Well, it certainly takes all sorts to make a world, doesn't it,' said Mabel disapprovingly. 'Imagine anyone getting into such a state. I'm not going to bother Mr. Scrope with nonsense like that when he comes back; it wouldn't mean a thing to him. Just forget it, Perce.'

And Percy agreed that that was the only thing to do.

Chapter Eight

In English villages as small as Mellingham-in-the-Vale, which was so small that the post office sold sweets and balls of worsted and there was only one oasis, the Goose and Gander, where you could get a drink, the man who matters is always the owner of the big house. It is he who, even if he is a Crispin Scrope, is supposed to have a head wiser than the ordinary; it is to him that the residents bring their problems and grievances.

As Constable Ernest Simms, the local police force, was about to do on the day following Crispin's return from London. He trudged up the drive of Mellingham Hall, an impressive figure well calculated to strike terror into the hearts of evildoers, and was admitted by Crispin's butler, at whom he cast a stony look, returned with one even stonier. They were not on good terms.

'Hullo, ugly,' said the butler. 'And what might you be wanting?'

'Not any of your impertinence,' was the frigid reply. 'I wish to see Mr. Scrope.'

'Does he wish to see *you*,' said the butler, 'that's the question. All right, go on up and spoil his day. He's in the library.'

The library was on the second floor, a large sombre room brooded over by hundreds of grim calf-bound books assembled in the days when the reading public went in for volumes of collected sermons and had not yet acquired a taste for anything with spies and a couple of good murders in it. It had always oppressed Crispin, but it had this one great advantage, that it was never invaded by paying guests. Once there, a man could meditate without fear of interruption.

A recent financial venture from which he was hoping that large profits would result had provided Crispin since his return with much food for meditation. Inflamed by Barney's enthusiasm for its prospects and telling himself that if you do not speculate you cannot accumulate, he had placed one hundred pounds of his brother Bill's two hundred and three pounds six shillings and fourpence on the nose of the horse Brotherly Love in the coming two-thirty race at Newmarket.

He had told Barney that he did not bet nowadays, but this could scarcely be described as a bet, so certain was the outcome. Consider the facts. Not only had Willoughby just given a notable example of brotherly love, but the animal was owned by a man he had been at school with and was to be ridden by a jockey whose first name was Bill. What redblooded punter could have been expected to ignore a combination of omens so obviously proceeding from heaven?

And the seal was set on his confidence when Constable Simms entered, for the surname of the jockey whose parents had christened him Bill was Copper. Really, it seemed to Crispin, it was hardly worthwhile going through the formality of running the race. It would be simpler if his turf accountants just mailed him their cheque right away.

'Come in, Simms, come in,' he cried sunnily. 'You want to see me about something?'

The officer gave no outward indication of sharing his exuberance. His aspect was grave. He looked, as always, as if he had been carved from some durable form of wood by someone who was taking a correspondence course in sculpture and had just reached his third lesson.

'Yes, sir,' he replied, and his voice was curt and

official. One would have said that he was anxious to impress on his overlord that this was no mere social visit. 'It's with ref to your butler, sir.'

Crispin's cheerfulness diminished sharply. The word seemed to have touched an exposed nerve. A moment before, he had been glad, glad, glad, like a male Polyanna: this ebullience no longer prevailed. He looked anxious and wary.

'My butler?' he echoed. 'What's he been doing?'

Ernest Simms's manner took on the portentousness which always came into it when he gave evidence in court.

'It has been drawn to my attention that he inaugurates games of chance at the Goose and Gander, contrary to the law. When I warned him that if he persisted in these practices I should be compelled to take steps, he called me an opprobrious name.'

Having given his audience time to shudder, he resumed, and it seemed to Crispin that he was changing the subject, for his next words took the form of a statement that yesterday had been his mother's birthday.

'She lives at Hunstanton in Norfolk, and I always send her a telegram on her birthday.'

Crispin continued fogged. At the sentiment behind this filial act nobody could cavil, for a policeman's best friend is admittedly his mother, but he could think of nothing to say except possibly that it did him credit. He remained silent.

'I went into the post office, leaving my bicycle propped up outside, and despatched my telegram, and when I came out...' Here Ernest Simms paused and seemed to choke, as if, man of chilled steel though he was, his feelings had become too much for him. 'And when I came out,' he repeated, conquering his momentary malaise, 'there was that butler giving young Marlene Hibbs a bicycle lesson on *my* bicycle.'

This time Crispin felt obliged to comment, and it is a

matter for regret that his critique should have been so inadequate.

'He shouldn't have done that,' he said.

'You're right he shouldn't,' Ernest Simms agreed, speaking with the asperity of a man whose finest sensibilities have been outraged, 'and so I told him. I told him that bicycle was Crown property and when he gave girls rides on it, he was deliberately insulting Her Majesty the Queen. I said if I caught him doing such a thing once again, I'd have him locked up so quick it would jar his back teeth.'

'That should have impressed him.'

'It didn't. He talked about being fed up with police persecution. And he uttered threats.'

'Threats?'

'Yes, sir, threats. He said he'd get even with me. He said he'd make me wish I'd never been born.'

'I don't like that.'

'Nobody would like it, sir, particularly with that Marlene Hibbs standing by and laughing fit to split.'

'Tut.'

'You may well say "Tut", sir. Not to mention making allusions to the Gestapo and calling me the fuzz, which is an expression she must have picked up at the cinema.'

'Monstrous,' said Crispin, 'monstrous. But what can I do?'

'Dismiss him from your service, sir. He is a disruptive element.'

It was a policy which Crispin would have been most happy to pursue, but there were reasons, impossible to explain, why he was not at liberty to dismiss butlers from his service. All his sympathies were with Ernest Simms, but he was hampered, handicapped and helpless.

'Well, I'll speak to him,' he said, and was conscious even as he spoke how weak it sounded.

That the constable had formed a similar opinion was made plain by the stiffness of his attitude as he took his departure.

'Very good, sir,' was all he said, but if he had added, 'And I suppose I ought not to have expected anything better from a worm like you', he would not have made his sentiments clearer.

Having given him plenty of time to leave, Crispin went out on to the drive, where he paced up and down, musing on the recent interview. It was a risky thing to do, for out in the open like this he was in grave danger of being buttonholed by his paying guests, by Colonel Norton-Smith, for instance, with his fund of good stories of life in the Far East or R. B. Chisholm, who held gloomy views on what was to become of us all if things went on the way they were doing; but he needed air and, like Jerry, thought better when in motion.

He was anxious to find a solution for the problem of what precisely his employee had had in mind when predicting that he would make Ernest Simms wish he had never been born. It might be this or it might be that, but whatever the inner meaning of the words they plainly implied some form of activity of which he would be bound to disapprove. If there is one thing at which a peaceable householder looks askance, it is the prospect of his butler making the police wish they had never been born, and it is not to be wondered at that Barney, coming out of the house, saw at once that all was not well with her host and being the kindly soul she was proceeded to make enquiries.

'Something wrong?' she said.

Crispin started with all the animation of a Mexican jumping bean, but recognizing who it was that had spoken immediately became calmer. To Barney's company he had no objection; indeed he welcomed it. Since that first meeting in Willoughby's office he had grown very fond of her. He felt it would be a relief to confide in her his fears and misgivings. When, therefore, she repeated her question, he did not brush it off with a 'No, no, nothing', as he would have done had his inquisitor been Colonel Norton-Smith or R. B. Chisholm. Coming, as the expression is, clean, he said:

'Yes, I am extremely worried, Mrs. Clayborne.'

'Barney.'

'Yes, I am extremely worried, Barney. A most unpleasant situation has arisen.'

'That's bad. We don't want unpleasant situations arising, do we? Who's been doing what?'

'It's Chippendale.'

'Who?'

'My butler. His name is Chippendale.'

A less considerate woman, given such an opening for the exercise of wit, would have asked: 'Has he made any good chairs lately?', but Barney appreciated that this was no time for jesting. Her heart was touched by Crispin's obvious distress. What, she enquired, had Chippendale been doing?

It was not so much, Crispin said, what he had been doing, though that was calculated to make him a hissing and a byword at the bar of world opinion, as what he might be going to do in the near future. The whole story came pouring out, and Barney listened with the grave attention of a Harley Street specialist receiving the confidences of a patient. When it ended, she had reassurances to offer.

'I don't see where you have to worry. This Chippendale guy may talk big, but it's just a lot of hot air. Come right down to it, what can he do? How many policemen are there around these parts?'

'Only one.'

'Then I've seen him. He's as big as all outdoors, must weigh two hundred pounds, and Chippendale's a little shrimp who couldn't fight his way out of a paper bag. The thing would be over in the first round.'

'But suppose Chippendale lurks and does him some secret injury?'

'Such as?'

Crispin had to admit that he could not specify one offhand, and Barney said he must not let his imagination run away with him.

'You're thinking of what happens in these novels of suspense. You see him slipping cobras down the cop's chimney or adding some little-known Asiatic poison to his evening glass of beer. But if it gives you the jitters, him being here, why don't you simply ease him out? Nothing so difficult about firing a butler, is there?'

Crispin hesitated. We all have secrets which we prefer to keep to ourselves, and he saw that he was on the verge of revealing his darkest one. Then his need for sympathy overcame reticence.

'I can't fire him.'

'Why not?'

'Because he's not a butler.'

'He acts like one.'

'I mean not a real butler.'

'I don't get you.'

'He's employed by the firm that does the repairs about the house. I owe them a lot of money. It's been owing for two years. So they sent him down here, and I can't get rid of him till I pay them. He's what is called a broker's man. I don't know if you have them in America.'

Barney was not an easy woman to surprise, but she could not repress a startled ejaculation. It had never occurred to her that this sort of thing went on in the stately homes of England. Mellingham Hall had made a deep impression on her, and it came as a shock to learn that its cupboards were staffed with such unpleasant skeletons.

'You mean you're busted?'

'I don't know which way to turn.'

'Well, fry me for an oyster. I'd never have guessed it. No wonder you didn't want to put any money on Brotherly Love. What are you going to do about it?'

'I have no idea.'

'I have. You must marry somebody with lots of money.'

'Who would have a man like me?'

'With a place like this? Dozens. You've only to advertise in *The Times* that you're open to offers, and they'll come running. Good heavens, man, you're amiable, intelligent, understanding, sober, honest and kind to animals. I saw you talking yesterday to that cat that hangs around, and I could see you were saying all the right things. You'd be snapped up in no time. Then you'd be able to run this place as it ought to be run, and you could fire Chippendale. How come, by the way,' said Barney, seeming to feel, like the detective in a mystery story, that there were still some pieces in the jigsaw puzzle that had to be fitted into place, 'that this Chippendale character is buttling?'

'That was his suggestion. He said he supposed I didn't want my paying guests to know why he was here, so he would pose as the butler. I don't have to pay him anything.'

The gravity with which Barney had been discussing the secret life of the owner of Mellingham Hall gave way to mirth. She uttered a laugh which was probably audible in the next county.

'Then you're sitting pretty, seems to me. A non-profit-making butler who can't give notice, it would make the mouths of some of my Long Island buddies water. They have to slip theirs a prince's ransom every pay day, and they can never be sure when the fellows won't hear the call of the wild and resign their portfolios. So what are you fussing about? We've already decided that Chippendale's threats about what he's going to do to the cop can be written off. Just baloney. And he seems to buttle all right. Cheer up, Crips, and keep smiling. That's the thing to do. If you go through life with a smile on your face, you'll be amazed how many people will come up to you and say, "What the hell are you grinning about? What's so funny?" Make you a lot of new friends.'

This excellent advice, so simple and yet so practical, ought, one would have said, to have been acted on without delay by its recipient, but if Crispin proposed to go through life with a smile on his face, it was plain that he did not intend to start immediately. Nor did the emergence from the house at this moment of the resident broker's man do anything to improve his morale. It is possible that Chippendale had his little circle of admirers who brightened at the sight of him, but Crispin was not of their number.

'You're wanted on the telephone, sir,' said Chippendale. Had he and Crispin been alone, he would have used the less formal 'chum' or 'mate', but the presence of Barney restrained him. 'Says he's your brother.'

Crispin hurried into the house, followed by Chippendale, who made for the butler's pantry, where there was an extension. It was his practice to listen to all telephonic conversations, for you never knew when you might not pick up something of interest.

'Bill?' said Crispin.

'Is that you, Crips?'

'Your voice sounds funny, Bill. Is something the matter?'

'You're damned right something's the matter. That blasted Clayborne woman has stolen my Girl In Blue,' thundered Willoughby, and Chippendale's lips framed themselves in a silent 'Coo!'.

The lips of a more emotional man would have made it 'Gorblimey!'.

Chapter Nine

Willoughby had come back from his golfing holiday in the most jovial of spirits. His putting had been good: he had corrected, if only temporarily, the slice which had been troubling him for weeks: he had got a birdie on the long seventh; and the thought that Gainsborough's Girl In Blue would be awaiting him on the mantelpiece in his study set the seal on his euphoria. If ever a rather stout senior partner in a law firm came within an ace of singing like the Cherubim and Seraphim, he was that rather stout senior partner.

And now this had happened. How true is the old saying, attributed to Pliny than Elder, that a man who lets himself get above himself is simply asking for it, for it is just when things seem to be running as smooth as treacle out of a jug that he finds Fate waiting for him round the corner with the stuffed eelskin.

Turning to the other parties in the conversation which had so dramatically begun, Chippendale was listening with his ears pricked up like a Doberman pincher's, while Crispin stood rigid with amazement, the receiver trembling in his grasp. It was impossible for him to suppose that he had not heard correctly, for the speaker's voice had nearly cracked his eardrum. He could only think that his brother was labouring under some strange delusion. It was unusual for Bill to have strange delusions, but he refused to believe that a woman like Bernadette Clayborne could be guilty of the grave offence with which that stentorian voice had charged her. Nice girls, he reasoned, don't steal things, and if Barney was not technically a girl, she was unquestionably nice. His recent exchange of ideas with her had left him more convinced of that than ever.

'What?' he said, and never had more consternation, agitation, indignation and incredulity been condensed into the restricted limits of a monosyllable. 'Is this a joke, Bill?'

There was a brief interval here, probably occupied by Willoughby in foaming at the mouth. At its conclusion he assured Crispin that it was not a joke.

'It's gone. I went away for a few days, leaving it on the mantelpiece in my study, and when I got back it wasn't there.'

'Have you looked everywhere?'

This query, like the previous one, seemed to give offence.

'Don't talk as if I had mislaid my spectacles!'

'Did you say you had mislaid your spectacles?'

'No, I did not say I had mislaid my spectacles.'

'I'm always mislaying my spectacles.'

'Curse your spectacles!'

'Yes, Bill.'

This short digression on the subject of aids to vision seemed for some reason to have had a good effect on Willoughby, slightly restoring his calm. When he resumed the conversation, his voice, though still retaining something of the robustness of that of an annoyed mate of a tramp steamer, was quieter.

'What's the sense of asking if I'd looked everywhere? If you leave a miniature on a mantelpiece and it vanishes from the mantelpiece, somebody must have taken it.'

'It might be on the floor.'

'What do you mean it might be on the floor?'

'Fallen there. Sudden puff of wind.'

Even to Crispin this did not seem a very bright suggestion, and Willoughby's opinion of it was also low.

There was another silence. Eventually he spoke.

'Don't be an ass, Crips.'

'No, Bill.'

'Sudden puffs of wind!'

'I see what you mean, Bill. But why—'

'—do I think this woman has got away with it? Who else could have? I told you she and Pyle had been staying with me. You don't suppose a reputable corporation lawyer like Pyle would steal things.'

'Nor would a charming woman like Barney,' said Crispin with spirit.

'Charming woman, my foot. She's a snake of the worst type. I know she's got my miniature, and I'll tell you why. The night before they left I was showing it to them at dinner, and Homer Pyle, though he tried to be polite, was obviously not interested. Twice I caught him yawning. The blasted female, on the other hand gushed over it. Kept picking it up and fondling it and saying how cute it was. She must have made up her mind there and then that she was going to have it, and after we had all gone to bed she crept down and pocketed it. It's the only possible solution. And I want it back, dammit.'

'I can quite understand, that, Bill.'

'And I'm going to get it. And that's where you come in.'

'Me, Bill?'

'Yes, you. I didn't ring you up to hear you say how sorry you were and what a disagreeable thing to have happened and all that. I want action, not sympathy. She's taken that miniature with her to Mellingham. Go to her, tax her with her crime, and tell her that if she doesn't give it up immediately, you'll send for the police.'

'Oh, I couldn't.'

'Then search her room.'

'Oh, I couldn't.'

'Why not?'

'Oh, I couldn't.'

'Listen, Crips, I know you're always hard up. I'll give you a hundred pounds if you can choke my Girl in Blue out of her.'

A wave of horror and indignation swept over Crispin. He had the illusion that his hair, what there was of it, was standing erect on his head. Much as he liked gold, this offer of it now revolted him. He drew himself to his full height, a wasted gesture seeing that Willoughby was many miles away, and uttered another of his dramatic monosyllables.

'No!'

'Two hundred.'

'No! I am sorry, Bill, but I absolutely refuse to have any part in this. Mrs. Clayborne is a woman I respect and admire, and I positively decline to wound her feelings by bringing baseless accusations against her.'

'Baseless, did you say?'

'Yes, baseless. You have no reason whatsoever for your foul suspicions.'

'Except this, that she's a notorious shoplifter. You didn't know that, did you? There isn't a department store in New York where they don't have a special squad of detectives on duty when they see her coming along to do a bit of shopping. That's why she's over in England. She made America too hot for her.'

Crispin had heard enough.

'You ought to be ashamed of yourself, Bill. Goodbye,' he said coldly, and replaced the receiver with a bang.

2

For several minutes after he had put an end to this regrettable scene Crispin sat quivering as a man might who had come safe but shaken through a testing motor accident. His thoughts were for the most part chaotic, but he was conscious of a definite surge of gratitude to the late Alexander Graham Bell for having invented the telephone. Face to face with his forceful brother he could never have taken that splendidly firm stand. From boyhood up Willoughby had always dominated him, and only Mr. Bell's co-operation had kept him from doing so now. Thanks to that human benefactor's ingenuity in enabling the weak to triumph over the strong at long range, he had borne himself with a fortitude and dignity which would have won the plaudits of the most captious critic. (Chippendale had been greatly impressed. It had come as a complete surprise to him that Crispin had it in him.)

As the after-effects of the battle of wills began to wear off, feelings of a more tolerant nature took the place of the indignation with which he had been seething. He could see now that one must make allowances for Willoughby. It was monstrous that he should have let his bereavement carry him away to the extent of inventing all that wild stuff about shoplifting, but no doubt quiet reflection would make him see how mistaken he had been. One must, at any rate, hope so. There was no real vindictiveness in Willoughby, it was just that he sometimes spoke without thinking.

He had reached this charitable conclusion and was preparing to go out again into the afternoon sunshine, hoping for a resumption of his interrupted conversation with Barney, when the door opened and Chippendale came in.

Reminded by the sight of him that he had other troubles beside those arising from a brother's unchivalrous attitude towards a woman he respected and admired, Crispin regarded him without elation. The 'Well?' he uttered was entirely free from geniality. He had not forgotten that he had promised Ernest Simms that he would speak to this man on the subject of his misdemeanours, and the task was one from which his sensitive soul shrank. Speaking meant speaking severely, and he was good at that only over the telephone.

If Chippendale noticed any absence of warmth, it did not appear to distress him. He spoke as one old friend to another.

'Like a word with you, cully.'

'Don't call me cully!'

'No harm in being matey, is there, chum?'

In her recent remarks on this employee of the people who did the repairs about the place Barney had described him as a little shrimp, and any impartial observer would have felt bound to support her in this view. There were only some sixty-six inches of him, and in the opinion of most of those who knew him that was quite enough. He was not a physically attractive man. His complexion was muddy, his ears stuck out like the handles of an antique Greek vase, and he had the beak and eyes of a farmyard fowl. Seeing him, one wondered how Marlene Hibbs could enjoy his society, even though a free bicycle lesson went with it. That he was entrusted with responsible work by the firm he represented was presumably due to the fact that those who engage the services of broker's men place more value on intelligence than on comeliness.

'And don't call me chum,' said Crispin. 'What do you want?'

In his lighter moments Chippendale would have replied that he wanted ten thousand a year, a Rolls Royce, a villa in the South of France and a diamond tiara, but he was here on business.

'Just a brief word, mate,' he said. 'I must begin by saying that when you and your brother Bill were on the buzzer just now I happened inadvertently to be on the extension.'

Crispin quivered in every limb. Even his moustache became mobile. He found a difficulty in speaking, but after a moment managed it.

'How dare you listen to a private conversation!'

'And if you don't mind me saying so, cocky,' Chippendale proceeded, rightly taking the view that this, if a question, was merely a rhetorical one, 'you were a mug to tell him off the way you did. If a bloke offers you two hundred quid, the least you can do is be civil. Civility never hurt anyone. Costs nothing, as somebody said. I learned that in Sunday school.'

Having administered this rebuke, Chippendale took a chair and put his feet up on the table.

'You were right, though, in saying you wouldn't go to the dame and tax her with her crime,' he resumed. 'That wouldn't get you anywhere. All she'd have to do would be to deny it what's the word, begins with a c, categorically,' said Chippendale, modestly proud of the scope of his vocabulary, 'and then where would you be? Where's your evidence? But searching her room, that's another matter. When Bill suggested that, he was talking sense. And as you probably won't want to do it yourself, you not being used to that sort of thing, what you do is hand the job over to me. And you're in luck, because I'm an experienced searcher. Had a lot of practice when I was a nipper. Whenever Father won a bit on the dogs, he'd hide the stuff around the house so that Mother couldn't get her hooks on it, and Mother would pay me a small royalty on any of it I could find, and I always found most of it. It won't take me long to locate that miniature, whatever a miniature is, sort of a small picture, isn't it; they had some in the drawing-room of a house I was staying at last year, kept 'em in a glass case. I'll spot it all right. Just a matter of keeping one's eyes open. We now have to ask ourselves,' said Chippendale, this having been disposed of, 'a very important question. Is Bill good for two hundred quid? It's a lot of money, but from the tone of his voice he seems to be a man of substance. These rich blokes get a sort of something into the way they talk. Kind of an authoritative note, if you know what I mean, like a referee sending someone off the field at a football match. So we'll take it the two hundred's there all right and we can go ahead.'

Except for odd bubbling sounds from time to time, horror and indignation had held Crispin dumb during the course of this long and revolting soliloquy. He now found speech.

'You are not to search Mrs Clayborne's room!' he bleated, and Chippendale smiled indulgently. These novices! Always getting the wind up.

'I know what you're thinking, chum. You're saying to yourself Suppose something goes wrong and I get copped. Well, of course, if I did, the balloon would certainly go up all right. Everybody would be telling you to send for the police and have me bunged into the nick, and you'd say No, you didn't want to bung the poor barstard into the nick because maybe it's his first offence and he yielded to sudden temptation. And then they'd say Well, if you won't jug him, chuck him out, and you'd say I can't chuck him out, because he's here in an official capacity, and they'd say How do you mean, an official capacity, and then it would all come out about you having the brokers in and what that would do to your social prestige would be plenty. But don't you worry, cully, I won't be copped, not if you do your bit all right. Your job is to get the dame out of the way while I operate. You say to her "Let's you and me go for a stroll round the estate, baby," and off you go and I pop in. Nothing to it. Though it's a pity she's got a suite and not just a bedroom, because if it was just a bedroom, it'd be simple. I'd go straight for the top of the cupboard, because that's where women always put stuff they want to hide. With a sitting-room what you might call the scope of enquiry broadens. I may have to bust open drawers and what not. I must remember to take a chisel. And now,' said Chippendale, 'about the split. You providing the bloke who's putting up the money and me doing the active work, I'd suggest a straight fifty-fifty.'

All the nausea and loathing which had been accumulating in Crispin since this man's entry to the room came to a head. He would have given much to have been able to substitute for his customary bleat the organ tones of his brother Bill, but he did his best with what he had.

'I forbid you to go near Mrs. Clayborne's suite,' he came as close to thundering as his vocal cords would allow. 'Get out!'

Chippendale stared at him, amazed.

'You mean you won't sponsor the enterprise?'

'That is what I mean.'

'Not for all that lovely splosh?'

'Damn the lovely splosh.'

'The deal's off?'

'Yes, it is. Get out.'

'Cor chase my aunt Fanny up a gum tree,' muttered Chippendale. It was an expression habitual with him when, as now, he was too astounded to say anything else.

3

Had there been an auditor of the two conversations just recorded, an auditor capable of hearing what was said at both, he could scarcely have failed to be impressed by the nobility of Crispin's attitude throughout. Here, he would have murmured to himself, is a man so fiscally crippled that his home is bulging with broker's men and in order to continue functioning he has to borrow two hundred and three pounds six and fourpence from his brother Bill, yet when this same brother Bill offers him a colossal sum to accuse a woman of stealing a miniature, he refuses because she is a woman he respects and admires and he doesn't want to hurt her feelings. And when the tempter suggests searching her room and securing the miniature by stealth, he dismisses him haughtily from his presence, saying that nothing would induce him to countenance such an outrage. The age of chivalry is not dead, the murmurer would have murmured, realizing that it was just behaviour of this sort that used to get the Chevalier Bayard such rave notices in his day.

It is with regret, therefore, that the chronicler has to state that what had activated Crispin's iron stand was not exclusively the spirit of chivalry. Operating almost equally with it had been the invigorating knowledge that after Brotherly Love had gone through the formality of winning the two-thirty at Newmarket he would have no need of the two hundred pounds which had so excited Chippendale's cupidity. He would be richer by more than a thousand.

Certain, however, though he was that Brotherly Love would not fail him, he could not help feeling a little nervous. Accidents, he knew, did happen. Horses strained fetlocks or tripped over their feet, causing the most gilt-edged snips to come unstuck. Jockeys bumped into a competitor and got themselves disqualified. There was no end to the list of things that could go wrong.

His watch told him that the race must have been over more than an hour ago, and he chafed at the inconveniences of living in the country. In the old days in London he would have had the result from the ticker at his club in a few minutes. At Mellingham he would have to wait for the nine o'clock news on the radio, for after what had occurred he could scarcely ring Willoughby on the phone and ask for information.

Pacing the library floor, he felt stifled. He felt that he must get away and out into the open, even though this would involve looking at the lake, and he was making for the door, when it flew open as if struck by one of those hurricanes off the eastern coast of America which become so emotional on arriving at Cape Hatteras, and Barney came in.

'Still in here?' said Barney. 'Don't tell me Bill kept you on the phone all this while. What did he want?'

It was in the circumstances an awkward question, and the best reply Crispin could find was that Bill had not wanted anything in particular.

'Just yakking, eh? Just a couple of old biddies swopping gossip over the garden fence? Well, what I came for was to ask you if you'd care to come for a spin in Colonel Norton-Smith's car. He's driving me over to Salisbury to see the cathedral.'

The programme she outlined had little appeal for Crispin. Of all his paying guests Colonel Norton-Smith was the one whose society he least courted, and as for cathedrals he had always been able to take them or leave them alone. He condensed these sentiments into an 'I don't think I will, thanks', and when Barney urged him to be a sport, he said, 'No, I think I won't, thanks', and she went out with a genial 'Suit yourself, but you're missing the treat of a lifetime', to poke her head in at the door a moment later.

'Oh, by the way,' she said, 'you were smart not to have anything on that Brotherly Love horse I was telling you about. Came in second. I've just had a telegram.'

She disappeared again, and it seemed to Crispin that the library, hitherto static, had suddenly begun to to execute the once popular dance known as the Shimmy. If the Collected Sermons of Bishop Pontifex (Oxford University Press, 1839) had shot from their shelf and struck him on the occipital bone, he could scarcely have gasped, gurgled and tottered more noticeably. The realization that his hundred pounds, like so many hundred pounds of his youth, had gone down the drain and that now he would be unable to fulfil his obligations to the repairs people and rid himself of their man at Mellingham affected him with a combination of epilepsy and ague. He was suffering, oddly enough, that very sense of guilt and remorse which Bishop Pontifex on page eighty-three of his monumental work warns his readers will always be the wages of sin. Paraphrasing the Bishop, he says that if you sin, you will inevitably feel like something the cat brought in, and that was how Crispin felt.

How long it was before he recovered the ability to face the crisis and examine the situation in depth he could not have said, but eventually something like coherent thought returned to him and he bent his mind to a careful study of his predicament, employing all his brain cells to an endeavour to find a way out of it.

And in due course he saw that there was such a way. It was not one of which the Chevalier Bayard would have approved, but it looked good to Crispin. His views on how one should behave towards women one respected and admired had undergone a radical change.

He rang the bell.

'Chippendale,' he said, when that blot on the local scene presented himself, 'shut that door.'

Chippendale shut the door.

'I have been thinking over the suggestion you made just now, Chippendale, and I have come to the conclusion that if you really are confident that by searching Mrs. Clayborne's suite you will be able to secure my brother's miniature—'

'It's a snip, chum.'

'Then do so at your earliest convenience,' said Crispin.

Chapter Ten

For some considerable time after he had heard the
receiver replaced up at Mellingham Hall Willoughby
sat motionless, a brooding figure not unlike Rodin's
celebrated Le Penseur. He was blaming himself for
having wasted the price of a long-distance call on someone as unlikely to be of any help to him as Crispin. He
had always been fond of Crispin, but he was not blind
to the fact that in any sort of emergency he was the
weakest possible reed on which to lean. Even had he
reacted favourably to the recent S.O.S., nothing con-
structive would have been accomplished. Crispin, as
Barney had said, was amiable, sober, honest and kind
to animals, but as a recoverer of stolen miniatures he
simply did not qualify. Not that one could blame him
for this. Some men have the knack of recovering stolen
miniatures, others not. It probably has something to do
with the hormones.

For such a task, Willoughby felt, you wanted someone younger, brighter and less prone, when a situation
called for decisive action, to stand about with his mouth
open and a glassy look in his eyes; someone, for
instance, like Archie Goodwin in the Nero Wolfe
stories, one of which he had been reading on the train,
or, it suddenly occurred to him in a flash of inspiration,
like his nephew Gerald.

Willoughby, though careful not to show it, for he
believed in keeping Youth in its place, had always had
an admiration for Jerry, the natural admiration of a

golfer whose handicap is a shaky eighteen for one who is plus two and plays in amateur championships. And while skill with driver and putter does not necessarily guarantee proficiency in other directions, it at least implies a steady nerve and the ability to concentrate on the job in hand, both of which qualities were demanded by the delicate operation he was planning.

Men like Willoughby make their decisions quickly. They do not sit humming and hawing and telling themselves they must look at a thing from every angle. Scarcely had the thought of Jerry entered his mind when he was on the telephone again.

'Jerry?'

'Oh, hullo, Uncle Bill.'

'You busy?'

'No.'

'Can you come round here?'

'To the office?'

'No, the house.'

'All right.'

'Well, hurry.'

Willoughby did not have to wait long. Jerry lived in one of the streets off the King's Road, a short step from Chelsea Square, and a talk with his uncle was just what at the moment he desired most, for it was his intention to put a quick end to all this nonsense of trusts and trustees. He would demand his money from him and thus become, if not financially equal to the girl he loved, at least a reasonably respectable suitor at whom the world could not sneer.

Vera Upshaw had pointed out how it could be done. Nothing could be simpler. You went to your Uncle Bill and you said to him, very correct and dignified but icily firm, 'Uncle Bill, I would have you know that I have examined the original indentures and I find that this trust is neither perpetual nor irrevocable but can be terminated by mutual agreement, so wash the damn thing out right away, or I get a complaint and summons and have them served.'

Not immediately, of course. You don't walk into a man's house and start crushing him beneath the iron heel without so much as saying Hullo. Obviously there would have to be a few preliminary pourparlers just to get things going, Uncle Bill being a good old scout with whom your relations had always been of the friendliest. So the first minutes of the meeting were taken up with a certain amount of Did-you-have-a-good-time-at-Sandwich-ing and How-was-your-slice-ing, and it was not till Willoughby had shown with a pair of tongs and a piece of coal how he had sunk that long putt on the sixteenth that Jerry was able to strike the business note.

'About that Trust, Uncle Bill.'

'Yes, that's what I wanted to see you about,' said Willoughby, 'I'm terminating it. You'll get the money next week.'

Jerry did not reel, but he certainly would have done so if he had not been sitting at the moment in a deep arm chair. His emotions were rather similar to those of Crispin when Willoughby had written the cheque for two hundred and three pounds six shillings and fourpence without a word of protest, joy at the happy ending competing with something that was almost disappointment that all the arguments and reasonings which he had so carefully rehearsed would now not be needed. Then, as in the case of Crispin, joy prevailed, and he expressed it with the quick sharp snort of ecstacy with which he was accustomed to greet the falling of his ball into the hole at the end of a thirty-foot putt. He found himself at a loss for words, and as he struggled to express his gratification Willoughby proceeded.

'You have probably been wondering why your father ever started the trust. Why didn't he let you have the stuff right away? Must have puzzled you, that.'

Jerry admitted that it had perplexed him.

'How well up are you on his early history?'

'I've heard that he didn't amount to much till he was thirty.'

'It's what he did when he was twenty-two that concerns us. He married a cinema usherette with a taste for drink. This was before he married your mother.'

'Are you saying he was a bigamist?'

'Certainly not. After making his life extremely unpleasant for a couple of years his bride handed in her dinner pail. And the experience gave him an obsession about early marriages. He took the view that all men under the age of thirty are halfwits and liable to charge into matrimony at the drop of a hat with the first tramp they come across, and he wasn't going to have that happen to you. So he formed this trust, putting me in charge and giving me the power to slip you the cash if I saw fit. Knowing that I wouldn't see fit if I saw you trying to head for the altar with somebody unsuitable, which of course is what happened. Vera Upshaw might be all right for a particularly well-to-do millionaire, but not for you. She wants a husband who will cover her with jewels and Rolls-Royces. Given those, she might make a good wife, though I would hesitate to bet on it. The engagement's really off, is it?'

'Yes, thank God.'

'You feel as I do that it was a merciful release? Quite right. Always bear in mind that however beautiful a girl may be, and I willingly stipulate that Vera Upshaw is scenically in the top ten, it's unwise to marry her if she has feet of clay. I became aware of such feet in Dame Flora Faye twenty-five years ago, and Vera is training on to be another Dame Flora Faye, and looks like making it. Did the betrothal end with a bang or a whimper?'

'I'd call it more of a coo. Her mother rang me up and filled me in. What a lovely voice she has.'

'Very musical. I remember it from the old days. What

94

did she say?'

'There was a whole lot of it, but what it amounted to was that Vera had changed her mind.'

'Which, translated from the Flora Faye, means that she has met someone with a lot more money than you.'

'You think so?'

'I am sure of it. It's a repetition of what happened twenty-five years ago with her mother and me. She doesn't mention it in her Theatre Memories as told to Reginald Tressilian, but at one time Flora and I were engaged. She chucked me for Charlie Upshaw, who had just come into the Upshaw's Diet Bread millions—most of which she spent years ago.'

A less perspicacious nephew might have murmured sympathetically, 'I see, I see. So that is why you have never married', and would probably have pressed his hand, but Jerry knew that his uncle's reason for remaining a bachelor was that he thoroughly enjoyed being a bachelor, that if he ever found himself at the altar rails it would be because he had been dragged there by wild horses, and that every time he thought of Charlie Upshaw he felt profoundly grateful to him for his kindly intervention. He contented himself with a word to the effect that the guardian angels of twenty-five years ago seemed to have been as efficient as those of today: and when Willoughby asked him what the hell he was talking about he explained that the Willoughby guardian angel had saved him from a union with Dame Flora Faye by producing Charlie Upshaw in the nick of time.

'While mine,' he added, 'arranged for Vera to meet this man you speak of who has a lot more money than me. And now that you have terminated the trust I am in a position to get some action with the girl I love.'

'Oh, my God. Are you in love again?'

'Yes, but this time it's the real thing.'

'Somebody unsuitable, of course?'

'On the contrary, she's a millionairess. And that was

95

the whole trouble, apart from being engaged to Vera. As long as I was poor I couldn't make a move, because you know what people think of a man without any money who goes after a girl with between one and two million. They sneer their heads off at him, taking it for granted that he's a contemptible fortune hunter who's simply out for a chance of getting a snug billet on Easy Street and three square meals a day.'

Willoughby's eyes widened. He was a man who could put two and two together, and the expression 'between one and two million', coupled with the recollection of Jerry's telephone call asking for her name, seemed to point in the direction of the late Mr. Donahue's heiress.

'Is it young Jane Hunnicut you're in love with?'

Amazement at his uncle's perspicacity held Jerry dumb for an instant, and Willoughby continued.

'But you've only met her once.'

'Twice actually, though once would have been enough.'

'Yes, I can see how it might. She's an attractive young prune.'

'Must you call her that?'

'Certainly I must. A girl is either an attractive young prune or she is not an attractive young prune. If she is an attractive young prune, why not say so? And she's got all that money.'

'If you knew how I wish she hadn't.'

'Yes, I believe you really do. But have you considered that it means that you're going to have a good deal of competition? Once the news of it gets around, contemptible fortune hunters with a taste for three square meals a day will start blooming like the flowers in Spring.'

'I know. That's why I've got to see her immediately.'

'But I'm afraid you can't. You're off this evening for Mellingham.'

'What! '

'Yes, I forgot to mention that there is a small condition attached to the termination of the trust. Before I hand you the cash I have a little job I want you to do for me. Do you remember that miniature I was showing you at that lunch?'

'The one of your great-great grandmother?'

'Or possibly great-great-great. Yes, that's the one, The Girl In Blue. And do you remember a Mrs. Clayborne who was at our lunch?'

'Of course. You called her Barney.'

'I'd hate to tell you what I'd like to call her now. She's pinched The Girl In Blue and taken it with her to Mellingham.'

'You're joking.'

'I wish I were.'

'But a woman like that can't be a thief.'

'That's what I said to her brother when he was warning me against her, and he told me that in New York department stores tremble like aspens when they see her coming their way, and I have no doubt her circle of friends always count the spoons carefully after they have had her to dinner. And even then I refused to believe that she would rob me when she was my guest and bursting with my salt. Had I but known, as they say in the mystery novels.'

Jerry was profoundly shocked. His acquaintance with Bernadette Clayborne had been only a brief one, but he had taken an instantaneous liking to her and even when confronted with evidence like this he could not believe in her guilt.

'But are you sure?'

'Of course I'm sure. Who else could have taken the thing? No, she's got it all right, and you're going to Mellingham to search her room.'

'Good Lord, I can't do that.'

'You'll have to if you want me to terminate the trust. I believe in reciprocity. Each helping each.'

'But I've got a dinner date with Jane Hunnicut on Saturday.'

'It'll have to be postponed. Send the girl a wire saying you have been suddenly called away to the country.'

'I don't know her address.'

'I've got it at the office. Write out the wire and I'll send it off tomorrow morning.'

'I don't know how to search a room.'

'You'll pick it up as you go along. For heaven's sake stop making all this heavy weather over an absurdly simple task well within the scope of a mentally retarded child of six. You'd think I was asking you to climb Mount Everest. You ought to be able to go through Barney Clayborne's effects in twenty minutes.'

A strong suspicion presented itself to Jerry that this was an underestimate, and his flesh crept briskly at the thought of what awaited him at Mellingham Hall, Mellingham-in-the-Vale, telephone number Mellingham 631, but he could see that it was useless to oppose his uncle's wishes.

'All right,' he said tonelessly.

'Splendid,' said Willoughby. 'There's an excellent train at about seven. I'll tell Crispin to expect you.'

Chapter Eleven

Jerry caught the excellent train without any difficulty, and on the following afternoon Vera Upshaw returned from Brussels, her lips tightly set and a frown on her lovely forehead.

It was only on very rare occasions that Vera frowned, for her mother had warned her that it led to wrinkles, but as she entered the flat in Eaton Square her brow was definitely knitted, and the discovery that Dame Flora Faye was out deepened her displeasure. Problems arise in a girl's life which only a heart-to-heart talk with an understanding parent can solve, and one of these had been vexing her for some days.

Fortunately before any great progress had been made by the wrinkles a latch key clicked in the door and Dame Flora came in, and having greeted her child sank into a chair with the announcement that her little body was a-weary of this great world.

'One of those ghastly literary lunches,' she explained. 'I don't know why I go to them. It isn't as if I were like Jimmy Fothergill, fighting for a knighthood and not wanting to miss a trick. This one was to honour Emma Lucille Agee, who wrote that dirty novel that's been selling in millions in America. Her publishers got up the lunch as part of the campaign for inflicting it on England. Chicken vol-au-vents, fruit salad and about fifteen of the dullest speeches I ever heard. The Agee woman told us for three quarters of an hour how she came to write her beastly book, when a simple apology was all that was required, and Jimmy replied for the visitors, which alone would have been enough to give the show a black eye, and eventually we were allowed to totter out into the sunshine. But why am I telling you all this, as I have so often said to subhuman leading men somewhere in the second act? It's the story of your life I want to hear. What have you to report?'

'Nothing.'

'Nothing?'

'Well, I saw Brussels and lots of delegates from the Balkans, and there was a charabanc expedition to Malines and a carillon concert and an inspection of Antwerp harbour by motor launch and a state banquet—'

'Don't be an ass, my chickabiddy. You know what I mean. You got my cable saying that I had given your house painter his two weeks' notice: go on from there. Get to what I may loosely call the love interest. Am I about to lose a daughter but gain a son? By the way, I met a man at the reception at the American Embassy the other night who knows all about Homer Pyle, and he said that any time Homer makes less than a hundred and fifty thousand dollars a year he clicks his tongue and mutters "Why this strange weakness?". You could be very happy on a hundred and fifty thousand dollars a year.'

Vera laughed the bitter little laugh with which she had greeted the statement that the Flannery and Martin book shop had not got a copy of *Daffodil Days*.

'I could,' she agreed, 'but it doesn't look as if I were going to be given the opportunity.'

Dame Flora uttered what in a less musical voice than hers would have been a blend of snort and squeak. Even when registering it on the stage she had never given a more convincing exhibition of incredulity.

'Are you telling me that I was all wrong about Homer Pyle, that those melting looks he was giving you meant nothing?'

'Apparently.'

'It isn't possible. I know what the trouble was. There were too many people around. How can you expect a man to turn the conversation to bridesmaids and wedding cake when he's up to his knees in Balkan delegates all the time? I can see what happened. Just as he was about to pour out his heart there would be a cheery "Hullo there" and another Balkan delegate would come muscling in. He might as well have tried to propose to you in Piccadilly Circus.'

Vera was not to be comforted. The pep talk was good, but it left her cold.

'We were alone and uninterrupted plenty of times. We dined together every night.'

'And nothing happened?'

'Nothing.'

'Well, you could knock me down with a lipstick,' said Dame Flora. 'I just don't understand it.'

And yet the explanation was quite simple. What neither had taken into consideration was the fact that Homer all his adult life had suffered from a marked inferiority complex where women were concerned. He was a modest man. He had no illusions regarding himself. He knew all about his horn-rimmed spectacles, his globular face and his dullness, and it seemed to him that he had no qualities to compensate for these. He had no doubts whatsoever of his wish to share his life with Vera Upshaw, but he lacked the audacity to ask her views. Swineherds in fairy stories probably had the same misgivings when they fell in love with princesses.

The trouble with making a steady hundred and fifty thousand dollars year after year—as a matter of fact with Homer it was nearer two hundred thousand—is that a man tends to take it for granted and not look on it as an asset. Homer was vaguely aware that there were women to whom his wealth would be an attraction, but he knew that it would carry no weight with one as spiritual as the author of *Daffodil Days* and *Morning's At Seven*. That was why he did not speak his love but let concealment like a worm i' the bud feed on his damask cheek, with the result that Vera Upshaw was getting wrinkles in her forehead and Dame Flora Faye was liable at any moment to be knocked down with a lipstick.

'I am dining with him tonight,' said Vera despondently, 'and I have no doubt he will continue to talk of the value to international understanding of these P.E.N. outings and what interesting people one meets on them. He won't get more personal than that. And tomorrow he leaves for the country to see his sister. She's staying at a place called Mellingham Hall in Hampshire or Sussex or somewhere.'

She broke off. Her mother had uttered a sudden cry which rang through the room like a war whoop.

'What was that name again?'

'Mellingham Hall.'

'Then there's still hope.'

'What do you mean?'

Dame Flora's eyes were sparkling as they had so often sparkled when she won an argument at rehearsals with a director.

'Listen, baby. Everything's going to be fine. I know Mellingham Hall. Bill Scrope took me there for the week-end twenty-five years ago. It belongs to his brother. It's the romantic spot to end all romantic spots, one of those old-world places full of shady nooks and secluded walks which were in operation when knights were bowled over by the local damsels. Well, when I tell you that it was there I met your father and we hadn't strolled together in a couple of shady nooks before he was asking me to be his, you'll understand what I mean. It was a bit awkward,' said Dame Flora meditatively, 'because I was engaged to Bill Scrope at the time and your father was engaged to somebody whose name I've forgotten, but these things can always be adjusted with a little tact. Believe me, honeybunch, you won't have any trouble with Homer Pyle once the Mellingham Hall atmosphere starts to work on him.' She paused, a look of disappointment on her face. 'You don't seem very exhilarated,' she said. 'Why aren't you clapping your little hands and dancing Spring dances all over the room?'

Vera's reaction had indeed lacked the animation a mother had the right to expect.

'It's a wonderful idea,' she said unemotionally. 'I was only thinking that you had overlooked one small point. How am I to get into this Mellingham Hall? I can't just walk in and say "Hullo there" like a Balkan delegate.'

Dame Flora would have none of this defeatism.

'Certainly you can if you pay the entrance fee. Didn't I mention that? Bill Scrope's brother, once opulent, is now hard up and takes in paying guests. He'll lay down the red carpet for you.'

Vera's despondency vanished as speedily as her mother's had done. There was no reason now to complain of any lack of enthusiasm on her part. It was in a very different tone that she repeated her remark that the idea was a wonderful one.

'But I can't go for a few days. I must buy dresses and things.'

'Buy all you want, my dream girl,' said Dame Flora cordially. 'Let there be no stint. Our aim is to knock Homer Pyle's eye out.'

2

While Homer with his failure to co-operate was giving Vera and her mother such cause for concern, the eccentric behaviour of G. G. F. West was proving an equal source of annoyance to Jane Hunnicut. His telegram cancelling the dinner to which she had been looking forward so eagerly, without a word of explanation except that he was going to the country, had left her, as the expression is, fuming. She was a sweet-tempered girl—you have to be to keep smiling at the Mr. Donahues who travel by air—but she was conscious of a well-defined urge to hit him on his ginger head with a brick.

Why the country? What did he want to go to the country for? Whereabouts in the country? How long was he going to be in the country? It occurred to her that there was an authority who could probably give the answer to these questions, his uncle Willoughby. Telephoning his office, she was told that he had left, presumably to go home. She took a taxi to 31 Chelsea Square, still fuming.

Willoughby was in his study, a cigar between his lips and a refreshing whisky-and-soda at his side. He was re-reading a letter which had come for him that morning from his nephew Gerald. He had read it twice in the course of the day, and each time, except for the postscript, with the same feeling of satisfaction. It is always gratifying to an executive to know that the subordinate to whom he has entrusted a delicate commission is proving himself worthy of his confidence.

'Things' (Jerry wrote) 'ought to be beginning to move soon. Yesterday and today it has been raining all the time and Mrs. Clayborne hasn't stirred from her sitting-room, so of course I couldn't do anything, but I heard her tell Uncle Crispin that she was going to the village tomorrow to have tea with the vicar, with whom she has apparently got matey. As soon as she is out of the way I shall start my search. Her having a suite will make it more difficult, because there are so many more places where one has to look, but if she's swilling tea at the vicarage I shall have plenty of time.

'I still think you must be mistaken in supposing she was the one who swiped your miniature. She is a charming woman. The first thing she did when I arrived was to kiss me on both cheeks and tell me to call her Barney. She said she hoped I had recovered from that lunch, and she asked most affectionately after you. She may be a shoplifter, though you've probably got the story all wrong, but I'll swear she isn't the sort to pinch things from a house where she's staying as a guest. However, you sent me here to search her room, so I'll search it.

'It's a long time since I was at Mellingham, but it seems much the same, except that I think Uncle Crispin is going off his onion. He acts as if he had something on his mind and starts at sudden noises. Yesterday I came into the library and he was standing there in a sort of trance and didn't see me, and when I cleared my throat preparatory to saying Well, the rain didn't seem to show any signs of stopping, or something bright of that sort, he shot up like a rocketting pheasant and nearly bumped his head against the ceiling. He has also engaged the most extraordinary butler, a man of the name of Chippendale who calls one 'chum'. I suppose you have to take what you can get nowadays, but when I look at Chippendale and remember the stately major domos of my childhood and boyhood, I feel like turning my face to the wall.

'P.S. (wrote Jerry) Don't you think the miniature might be in your study somewhere? A puff of wind might have blown it to the floor. Have you looked everywhere?'

It was as Willoughby finished reading this postscript and was thinking that in the matter of weakness of intellect his nephew Gerald had much in common with his brother Crispin that Jane arrived.

He greeted her cordially. He had become very fond of her in the course of their brief acquaintance. Girls of her age group he tended as a rule to shun, but there was something about her that had appealed to him from the first.

'Come in and take a seat, drunken sailor,' he said welcomingly. 'And if my form of address puzzles you, I had in mind the way you've been spending money since you hit the jackpot.'

The charge had substance. Her sudden access to wealth had left Jane dizzy, but not so dizzy as to be unable to go through London's emporia like a devouring flame. Her expenditure guaranteed by the firm of Scrope, Ashby and Pemberton, she had bought several dresses, several hats, an expensive car and some nice bits of bijouterie in Bond Street. Willoughby's comparison of her to an inebriated seaman on shore leave was not inaccurate. Writers through the ages have made a good many derogatory remarks about money, and one gets the impression that it is a thing best steered clear of, but every now and then one finds people who like the stuff and one of these was Jane. It seemed to her to fill a long-felt want.

'I suppose you've come now,' said Willoughby, 'to tell me you've decided to buy an estate in the country and you want Scrope, Ashby and Pemberton to advance the cash for it. If so, let me recommend Mellingham Hall, Mellingham-in-the-Vale. Desirable Elizabethan residence, gravel soil, company's own water, spreading parklands and a lake. And I believe my brother Crispin could be induced to sell.'

Jane promised to bear it in mind.

'But at the moment,' she said, 'all I want from Scrope, Ashby and Pemberton is information concerning G. G. F. West.'

'What do you want to know about him?'

'Where he is, and what he means by going there when we were supposed to be having dinner together tomorrow night. It was all set, and I get a telegram from him saying it's off because he's gone to the country.'

'Yes, to my brother's house, the one you're going to buy. He left very suddenly.'

'But why? When we had this dinner date.'

'On a diet perhaps, do you think? Fleeing from temptation.'

Jane uttered a cry. A bright light had flashed upon her. She eyed Willoughby narrowly.

'Did you tell him about my money?'

'I did. Why not?'

'Then I see what's happened. He's got scruples about marrying a rich girl and, as you say, is fleeing from temptation.'

'As in the stories in women's magazines?'

'Exactly. Don't you think I'm right?'

'I shouldn't wonder. He's ass enough for anything.'

'Mr. Scrope, you are speaking of the man I love.'

'Oh, you do love him?'

'Of course I do. Who wouldn't?'

'I for one. He writes people letters with idiotic post-scripts. But I'm glad to hear you love him, because he loves you. He told me he did.'

'Of course he does. I can see it in his eye. But he has these scruples.'

'Yes, he told me that, too.'

'What an ass!'

'Miss Hunnicut, you are speaking of the man you love.'

'And yet there's something sweet and wonderful and beautiful about it, don't you think?'

'No.'

'I mean there aren't many men who would let their scruples stand between them and a million dollars.'

'That's because most men have sense.'

'Of course you've only got to look at him to see the sort of man he is. Don't you think he's got lovely eyes?'

'No.'

'What was he like as a little boy?'

'Horrible.'

'Well, there's only one thing to be done. I must go to

this Mellingham place and overcome those scruples. Can you give me a letter of introduction to your brother?'

'It won't be necessary. He takes in paying guests.'

'How very convenient. So I just ring the front door bell and walk in?'

'Exactly.'

'Goodbye then, Mr. Scrope. I won't take up more of your valuable time.'

'Always a pleasure to see you. Drop in again if you want to buy Buckingham Palace or anything like that. Scrope Ashby and Pemberton are always at your service.'

For some moments after Jane had left, Willoughby, with a new cigar and another whisky-and-soda, sat bathed in the sentimental glow which comes to elderly bachelors when they hear stories of young love. Much though he himself disapproved of marriage, he was broadminded and could appreciate that others might feel differently about it, and it was pleasant to think that his nephew was going to link his lot with that of a millionairess, for he had no doubt that Jane Hunnicut would be successful in her efforts to hammer sense into Jerry. His acquaintance with her had left him with the conviction that she was a girl who, like the Canadian mounted police, would not fail to get her man.

Good luck to her, he was saying to himself, when a disturbing thought intruded. Would her advent divert Jerry's thoughts and take his mind off his sacred mission?

His apprehension did not last long. A clear-thinking man, he saw that he was disturbing himself unduly. Those scruples of which they had been speaking made it essential for Jerry that he deliver the goods and so lift himself out of the poor suitor class by obtaining the trust money. Jane's presence would act as a stimulus, urging him on to give of his best and rise to new heights of endeavour. It was with restored composure that he reached for the telephone.

'Crips?'

'Oh, hullo, Bill.'

'Just wanted to tell you, Crips, that I'm sending you another guest, a girl called Hunnicut, who's a friend of Jerry's. And don't say "Oh, Bill!" like that, as if I were reporting the death of a favourite aunt. Yes, I know you don't want girls about the place, but this one is special. She's just come into an enormous fortune and is buying up everything in sight. There's quite a chance, if you play your cards right, that she will take the Hall off your hands.'

3

The immediate effect of this announcement on Crispin was to extract from him a strangled gulp, the bronchial equivalent of Chippendale's 'Cor chase my Aunt Fanny up a gum tree'. For some moments his rigidity was so pronounced that he might have been mistaken for a statue of himself erected by a few friends and admirers. Then, as the full beauty of Willoughby's words penetrated to his consciousness, this inelasticity gave place to something resembling the animation of a war horse that has heard the sound of the bugle. The war horse, we are told, when the sound of the bugle is drawn to its attention, becomes a good deal stirred. It starts. It quivers. It paws the valley, rejoices in its strength and says 'Ha, ha' among the trumpets, and it was thus, give or take a 'Ha, ha' or two, that Crispin behaved.

Becoming calmer, he found doubts creeping in. Willoughby, he knew, was far too prone to say things in a spirit of jest and to joke on serious subjects. This might be merely his idea of humour. It was a paralysing thought, but there was a way by which the truth could be ascertained. Willoughby had spoken of this girl as a friend of his nephew Gerald. Gerald could provide official information concerning her financial standing. He went in search of him and found him in the billiards room practising moody canons.

'Gerald,' he said, making him miss an easy one, 'do you know a girl called Hunnicut?'

The cue fell from Jerry's grasp and clattered to the floor. He had an odd illusion that his heart had leaped from its moorings and crashed against his front teeth. It was as if the voice of conscience had spoken. Not for an instant since his callous cancelling of their dinner engagement had been free from a corroding sense of guilt. He saw himself as that lowest of created beings, the man who asks a girl to dinner and at the last moment stands her up. It was in his opinion the sort of thing that someone like Benedict Arnold would have done, and he was trying not to picture what Jane Hunnicut must be thinking of him.

'Willoughby,' Crispin continued, 'says she is coming here.'

Once again Jerry's heart executed a Nijinsky leap. He was finding Crispin hard to focus, and was obliged to blink several times before he could see him steadily and see him whole. His uncle seemed to be flickering like something in an early silent picture.

'Coming here?' he heard himself croak.

'And he says you know her.'

'Know her?'

'Yes,' said Crispin, justifiably irritated, for no uncle likes to converse with a nephew who models his conversation on that of an echo in the Swiss mountains. 'Know her. Do you?'

'Yes.'

'Is she rich?'

'Yes.'

'I mean *really* rich?'

'She has between one and two million dollars,' said

Jerry with a shudder.

'Ha!' said Crispin, as if he were saying it among the trumpets.

Jane arrived soon after lunch next day, but it was not for some little time that Jerry had the opportunity of an extended conversation with her. When Crispin received a guest who might take it into her head to buy Mellingham Hall, he received her thoroughly. Wherever Jerry went, he seemed to come on the two of them, Crispin prattling, Jane listening politely. It was only when Crispin was summoned by Chippendale to go indoors to take a telephone call, leaving them standing by the lake, that the interview which Jerry had been half dreading, half looking forward to was able to proceed.

Chippendale in his friendly way lingered long enough to give Jerry a cordial wink accompanied by a vertical raising of the thumbs, presumably to indicate that Jane had met with his approval, and seemed on the point of engaging them in amiable chat, but apparently thought better of it and withdrew, and they were alone except for a duck, remarkably like Chippendale in appearance, which was quacking meditatively in the water not far away.

If Jerry had attempted to open the conversation, he would probably himself have quacked, for he was deeply stirred and in no shape to frame a coherent remark. Although this encounter had not come on him as a surprise, it had done much to cause his vocal cords to seize up. It was Jane who spoke first.

'I seem to remember that face,' she said. 'Mr G. G. F. West, is it not?'

Mr. G. G. F. West still being in no condition to sustain his share of the exchanges, she continued.

'You are probably wondering what I am doing here. How the girl does flit about, you are saying to yourself, here today, Bournemouth yesterday, London the day before that, doesn't she ever stay put? The explanation is very simple. I felt that if Mellingham Hall was so irresistible that you couldn't keep away from it even though it meant breaking your sacred promise to take me out to dinner, it must be an earthly Paradise and I ought to come and have a look at it. And I must say it well repays inspection. But it's a shame about that dinner. From Barribault's point of view, I mean. They were expecting to clean up, for they knew that you would have spared no expense.'

Jerry found speech. Nothing very bright, but technically speech. He said:

'I'm sorry.'

'Me, too.'

'I was going to write to you and explain.'

'Take some explaining.'

'Only I can't.'

'I don't follow you.'

'I mean it's rather secret stuff. Can you keep a secret?'

'No.'

'You could try.'

'Oh, I'll try.'

'Well, then, it's like this.'

He told his story well, omitting no detail however slight, and she listened attentively. When he had finished, she gave her verdict as uncompromisingly as she had done after weighing the evidence in the case of Onapoulos and Onapoulos versus the Lincolnshire and Eastern Counties Glass Bottling Corporation.

'Your Uncle Bill is a hell hound.'

'No, he's all right.'

'Landing you with a job like that.'

'He wants that miniature rather badly.'

'I dare say, but I maintain that, slice him where you like, he's still a hell hound. Do you know what I would do if I had an uncle who wanted me to search people's rooms? I'd tell him to go to blazes. I'm surprised that you didn't.'

'I couldn't. There's the money.'

'Money isn't everything.'

'It is as far as I'm concerned. You see, I'm in love with a girl—'

'Well, that's always nice.'

'—and she's damned rich and I'm damned poor.'

'I don't see where that matters. If she's worth falling in love with, she won't mind.'

'It isn't her minding that's the trouble, it's me minding.'

'You don't want to seem a fortune hunter?'

'Exactly.'

'Has it ever occurred to you that you ought to be certified?'

'It has from time to time, and then from time to time it hasn't. I think on the whole I'm doing the sensible thing.'

'I don't. If the post of village idiot at Mellingham-in-the-Vale is vacant, I feel you ought to apply for it. Still, I suppose it's no good trying to reason with you. So what are your plans? When do you search?'

'This afternoon.'

'Golly!'

'Yes, that's rather how I feel. But it's got to be done.'

'What happens if she catches you?'

'I don't like to think of it. I'm hoping everything will be all right. She's having tea with the vicar. But you might be praying for me, will you?'

'If you think it would be helpful,' said Jane. 'It will have to be the one for those in peril on the sea, because that's the only one I remember.'

Having lingered to wink at Jerry and elevate his thumbs as a tribute to Jane, Chippendale had not been able to reach the extension in the butler's pantry in time to listen to Crispin's telephone call, but one is happy to say that he missed nothing that would have been worth hurrying for. It was only from the vicar thanking Crispin for his gift of two old pairs of trousers and a teapot with a cracked spout to the forthcoming Jumble Sale in aid of the Church Lads Annual Outing. There were, of course, a few words of pleasant conversation just to keep the thing from seeming abrupt. The vicar said how eagerly he was looking forward to enjoying Mrs. Clayborne's company at the tea table; a charming woman didn't Crispin think, and Crispin said Yes, charming, charming. Oh, and would Crispin tell her to be sure to bring with her that novel by Emma Lucille Agee, I think that was the name, of which she had spoken in such high terms, and Crispin said he would not forget, which he promptly did. Nothing, in short, which would have repaid Chippendale for the trouble of picking up the extension receiver.

It was perhaps an hour later, getting on for half-past four, that Crispin, returning to the library to avoid R. B. Chisholm, who wanted to talk to him about the situation in the Middle East, found Chippendale in a chair with his feet on a table, reading a book of sermons.

He seemed to be glad to be interrupted, though he was a man who sorely needed all the sermons he could get his hands on.

'Ah, there you are, cocky,' he said genially. 'Thought you'd be along sooner or later. Ever read this fellow? Canon Whistler he calls himself. Got a lot to say about hell fire. I suppose a clergyman had to in those days, if he wanted to keep his job. I've got a cousin who's a clergyman, well when I say a clergyman, he cleans out a church down Hammersmith way, dusts the pews and washes the floor and sees that the hymn books are all present and correct, makes a good job of it, too, the vicar calls him Tidy Thomas, that being his name, the same as mine only mine's Reginald Clarence. Shows what a small world it is.'

Crispin, lending a reluctant ear to these confidences, had made a discovery. He hastened to share this with his employee.

'Chippendale,' he said, 'you've been drinking.'

So manifestly true was this charge that the blush of shame would have mantled the cheek of a more sensitive man, but Chippendale acknowledged it with no change of colour. He did not go in much for blushes of shame.

'The merest spot, chum,' he said, 'the merest spot. I looked in at the Goose and Gander for a few quick ones, and do you know what Beefy told me?'

'Who the devil's Beefy?'

'Beefy Hibbs, the landlord, licensed to sell tobacco, wines and spirits. He's the uncle of Marlene Hibbs I gave a bicycle lesson to on Simms's bicycle, and he said Simms had been molesting Marlene.'

'Simms would never do such a thing.'

'Well, he did. She has a dog called Buster she dotes on, what you'd call the bull terrier type, and he accosted her in the High Street and told her in a very harsh manner that it had bitten him in the trouser leg, and when she pointed out that every dog is allowed a first bite by law, he said that if it happened again, he would prosecute it with the utmost severity and Buster wouldn't have a leg to stand on legally and would be for it. Hurt the poor child's feelings, as you can well imagine. I found her in tears by the village pump and had to stand her a strawberry ice cream before I could bring the roses back to her cheeks. The fact is the man's drunk with a sense of power and needs a sharp lesson, and I've thought of a way of giving it him if I can work it.'

Here was Crispin's opportunity to fulfil the promise he had made to Constable Simms that he would speak to Chippendale, but he let it pass. With so much on his mind he was incapable of interesting himself in the petty squabbles of these fretful midges. All that interested him was the question of Chippendale's ability to function as a searcher of rooms when he was so plainly under the influence of the wines and spirits which Mr. Hibb was licensed to sell.

He put this point to him with no attempt to spare his hearer's feelings with tactful circumlocution.

'How,' he asked, 'are you going to find that miniature when you're as tight as an owl?'

Chippendale weighed the question, and it amused him a good deal. He had to laugh like an entertained hyaena before he could reply. He knew that after those quick ones he was at the top of his form. Recovering his gravity, he admitted that he was perhaps a mite polluted, but ridiculed the suggestion that he was as tight as an owl.

'Just keyed up, chum. In the circumstances, if I may use the expression, a couple of snifters were unavoidable. You can't take on the sort of job I'm taking on without a little outside help. I remember when I was a nipper and used to go hunting for the stuff Father won on the dogs, I always had to have a swig of Mother's Vitamin B tonic to nerve me to the task. Don't you worry, mate. I'll deliver the goods all right. You stay here, cocky.' He wandered to the window, walking a little unsteadily. 'Ah,' he said, 'the dame has emerged and is navigating down the drive en route for the vicarage. The coast is clear. I'll be getting along and what's the word, begins with sub, no it's gone.'

He left the room, frowning thoughtfully, to return a moment later.

'Subject her belongings to the closest scrutiny,' he said. 'Knew I'd get it.'

5

He left Crispin a prey to the liveliest misgivings. He had had misgivings before in his time, but seldom any as lively as these. So much was at stake, and it was not agreeable to think that success or failure were in the wobbly hands of an agent who showed such unmistakable signs of having had what is technically known as one over the eight. His assurance that he was merely keyed up had done nothing to ease his mind. He clung to his original opinion that few owls could have achieved a more pronounced degree of tightness. And this being so, how would he comport himself in Mrs. Bernadette Clayborne's inner sanctum? Many workers sing at their work. What guarantee had he that Chippendale would not sing at his? Even now the suite might be ringing with drunken melody, and people pouring in from all directions to ascertain what was going on.

Calmer thoughts prevailed. Chippendale was a business man, counting on this venture to enrich him by a hundred pounds, and he would not allow the urge to warble to get the better of him. He would keep the thought of that hundred steadily before him and go through his task with his music still within him. And the vital thing was that there was no chance of an interruption by Barney. She had been seen going down the drive, heading on winged feet for the vicarage. Everything, in short, was perfectly all right, and like Kipling's soldier Crispin said to his fluttering heart strings 'Peace, be still'.

Nevertheless, a certain jumpiness still persisted, rendering it beyond his power simply to sit and wait for his agent's return from the front. 'You stay here, cocky,' Chippendale had said, and he had fully intended to do so, but the library with its hushed gloom was too much for him. He yearned for the great outdoors where there would not be seven or eight hundred bound volumes of early Victorian sermons eyeing him with silent rebuke. He rose and went down to the hall to get his hat, and was thus enabled to obtain an excellent view of Barney, who was coming in at the front door.

One of the less engaging qualities of the Gorgon of Greek mythology was, we are told, her ability to turn into stone anyone who was unlucky enough to catch sight of her, and it seemed to Crispin that this unexpected encounter with one who should have been tucking into tea and buttered toast at the vicarage had had a similar effect. It is a well-attested medical fact that the heart cannot take time off, but he would have required written proof to convince him that his own had not stopped beating.

He stood speechless, and Barney hailed him with her usual cheeriness.

'Hullo there, Crips. Came back to get a book I promised to lend the vicar. I left it in my room. I'll run up and get it.'

These were probably the only words in the language that could have unfrozen Crispin. They destroyed the faint hope he had entertained that the tea party had been called off and that it would be possible to persuade her to come for a walk.

'I'll get it,' he gasped.

'Nonsense,' said Barney. 'What do you think I am, a cripple? I can still manage a couple of flights of stairs.'

And she was gone, taking them two at a time, and Crispin, walking slowly like an Alpine climber climbing the Matterhorn, went back to the library. His aspect was that of one who has been looking for the leak in a gas pipe with a lighted candle. Another man in a similar situation might have been running what are called the gamut of the emotions, but he was conscious of only one, a dull despair. This, it seemed to him, was the end. He was not as a rule very imaginative, but there rose before him as clearly as if it had been the top line on an oculist's chart a vivid picture of what was going to happen next.

Barney, finding Chippendale subjecting her belongings to the closest scrutiny, was not the woman to refrain from comment. She would institute a probe or quiz, and Chippendale, grilled, would confess all, stressing his own position as that of a mere tool acting under the orders of the mastermind Crispin Scrope. The topic of the miniature would come up, she would stoutly deny ever having had it in her possession, and would probably sue him for defamation of character or slander or libel or whatever it was and be awarded heavy damages. At the best she would tell her story to the other paying guests and they would leave in a body. And while he was not fond of the other paying guests, he needed their money.

It was a situation that called for the burying of the face in the hands, and when he sat up after doing this he found that he had Chippendale with him.

From the point of view of an official of the Band of Hope or some other institution for promoting temperance Chippendale was in infinitely better shape than he had been on leaving the library. Then he had had the vine leaves in his hair and a drunken snatch on his lips. Now only an exceptionally abstemious Judge could have competed with him in sobriety. The Band of Hope official would have thought he looked fine.

A doctor, however, going deeper into the thing, would have realized that this transformation was the result of a shock and that a severe one, for his eyes were glassy, he breathed stertorously and he was perspiring in a manner which would have reminded a traveller in France of the fountains at Versailles.

'Cool' he said, and mopped his forehead.

'Cor stone the crows!' he said, and mopped it again.

'I don't want that one back,' he said. 'Have you ever been shut up in a small cage with a man-eating tiger?'

It so happened that Crispin had not, and he signified as much with a petulant shake of the head.

'What,' he asked, and would have added, 'happened,' but this voice failed him. Having gulped once or twice, he was able to articulate, though hoarsely. 'What happened?' he said.

'You may well ask, chum,' said Chippendale, continuing to mop. 'I have passed through the furnace, pal, but I came out unscathed, if that's the word, and I'll tell you why I came out unscathed. I came out that way because I've got presence of mind. Always have had from a child. Where others would have stood shuffling their feet with guilt written all over their ruddy faces, I kept my head and pitched a yarn and what's more made it stick. What would you have done if the dame had caught you in her boudoir same as she caught me? I'll tell you what you'd have done, cocky, you'd have reddened like a rose and swallowed your tonsils. You wouldn't have had a word to say. I, on the other hand—'

'Get on!' said Crispin.

'I, on the other hand, put a finger to my lips as she entered the room and whispered "'Ush!". I don't say she hadn't scared me out of a year's growth, because she had, but owing to this presence of mind I was speaking of I was enabled to up with my finger and put it to my lips and whisper "'Ush!". Naturally, being a woman, she didn't 'ush, but started asking questions. She wanted to know what I was doing there, giving me just the opening I required for telling the tale. Give you three guesses what I told her.'

'Get on!' said Crispin.

'I said I'd happened to be passing her door and chanced to hear noises within and being aware that she had gone off to revel at the vicarage I knew it wasn't her that was making the noises, so I deduced it must be a burglar, who had sneaked in and was going through her effects. To which she responded that I was barmy, because burglars don't burgle in the middle of the afternoon, and I said "Oh, don't they, that's where you make your ruddy error, because that's just when they do burgle, knowing that that's just when everybody's outside playing tennis and what not. You'll look silly," I said, "if you ignore my warning and persist in what's that word beginning with an s?"'

'Get on!' said Crispin. 'Get *on!*'

'Skip something, no not skip, skep. Sceptical, that's it. "You'll look silly," I said, "if you persist in this sceptical attitude and find later that the Clayborne diamonds have done a disappearing act. A proper mug you'll look, and no use then coming to me and expecting me to sympathize." This had her looking a bit more thoughtful. She chewed her lower lip. "Well, where is this burglar," she said. "Gone into the bedroom," I said, and she said, "Well, we might as well have a look there," so we went in and she said she didn't see any burglar, and I said, "Well, the window's open, isn't it, he's probably—" ... You haven't got a cigar, have you, mate? I need a sedative.'

Crispin produced his cigar case. Nothing could ever make him fond of Chippendale, but he was forced to admit that in a difficult situation he had shown considerable resource and deserved a reward. He had heard only a portion of the man's narrative, but already he was experiencing a delicious sense of relief, for evidently the subject of the miniature was not going to be touched on. Whatever turns and twists the conversation between Chippendale and Barney might take, that much seemed certain. So kindly did this make him feel that he not only gave the fellow a cigar but lit a match for him.

'Thanks, pal,' said Chippendale. 'I always find a

smoke soothes the nervous system. So where was I? Oh yes, in the dame's sleeping quarters, and she was saying "Well, where's your ruddy burglar?" and giving me the horse's laugh, when guess what. The cupboard in the corner of the room, which had hitherto not spoken, suddenly sneezed.'

'Good gracious!' said Crispin.

His unconcealed interest pleased Chippendale. Too often when he told a story his audience's only response was to urge him to put a sock in it, but here was someone he had really gripped.

'You may well say "Good Gracious", chum,' he said. 'It was roughly what I said myself. I don't mind telling you that sneeze went through me like a bullet through a pat of butter. I jumped a foot. The dame, on the other hand, remained unmoved. "Gezundheit", she said, but when I informed her that it hadn't been me, but the cupboard, she displayed immediate interest. "So there really is a burglar," she said, and I said, "Not only a burglar, baby, but a burglar with half an ounce of dust up his nose." And this is where she started to act like that tiger I asked you if you'd ever been shut up in a small cage with. She stiffened like a monarch of the jungle scenting its prey. This needs attending to promptly, she said, and she pops into the other room and comes back with a statuette that had been on the mantelpiece, a thing about a foot long with no clothes on, Shakespeare it may have been or Queen Victoria, and she whispers to me to open the cupboard door quick, which I done, revealing a bloke in a crouching posture, and she reaches in and lets him have it on the topknot with the statuette, using a good deal of follow-through, and he tumbles out, and it's that gingerheaded young fellow that blew in a couple of days ago, your nephew somebody told me he was, Best or West or something like that.'

'Gerald!'

'If that's his name.'

'But what was he doing in a cupboard?'

'I didn't stop to ask. I buzzed off. I wanted to be out of reach of that statuette, and the sooner the better. And what I looked in to tell you, cocky, was that as far as I'm concerned that enterprise we were discussing is off. I'll be losing money, but worse things can happen to you than not getting a hundred quid. Any further mucking about with the private apartments of a woman with a wallop like that you'll have to do yourself,' said Chippendale, blowing a smoke ring.

Chapter Twelve

Jerry, having parted from Barney and gone in search of Jane, found her outside the front door. She was standing by her car, and since he had last seen her she had changed her dress for something more ornate. This surprised him.

'Hullo,' he said. 'Are you off somewhere?'

'London. My New York lawyer has come over and wants to see me. He's just telephoned. Something about my legacy, I suppose. I'll be back this evening. But never mind that, I want to hear what happened. How did you get on?'

'Not too well.'

'I thought as much.'

It had not taken great perception to bring her to this conclusion. Even at a distance he would have struck her as being on the sombre side. To be obliged to retreat in disorder from a stricken battlefield always tends to lower the spirits. Napoleon, who had this experience at Moscow, made no secret of the fact that he did not enjoy it, and Jerry, going through the same sort of thing at Mellingham Hall, Mellingham-in-the-Vale, was definitely not at his perkiest. One glance had been enough to tell Jane that it was no tale of triumph that he had come to relate. Just so might a knight of old have looked when about to confess to his damsel that he had been unhorsed in the opening round of the big tournament.

'Something went wrong?'

'Everything went wrong.'

'My poor lamb!'

'She came in and caught me.'

'But she said she was going to the vicarage.'

'She must have changed her mind. If people who say they are going to the vicarage would only *go* to the vicarage, this would be a better and happier world,' said Jerry bitterly. The subject was one to which he had given much thought. 'She blew in before I'd had time to get really started.'

'What did you say?'

'I didn't say anything at the moment. I was hiding in a cupboard.'

'You were ... I don't think I got that.'

'I was in a cupboard, concealed.'

'Oh, I see. You heard her coming.'

'That's right.'

'And she looked in the cupboard?'

'Exactly.'

'What made her do that?'

'I sneezed. There's no need to laugh.'

'I wasn't laughing, just smiling. I was thinking of that thing in Alice In Wonderland. Speak roughly to your little boy and beat him when he sneezes. He only does it to annoy, because he knows it teases. Did she speak roughly to you?'

'As far as I can remember, there wasn't any conversation. She just biffed me over the head with some sort of statuette.'

'Golly!'

'And then she asked me what I was doing there.'

'An awkward question.'

'Very.'

'Difficult to find the right thing to say.'

'It did elude me for a moment. Fortunately I remembered I had been talking to her at lunch about a book she recommended highly. I said I had come to borrow it.'

'Explaining, of course, that when you borrow books you always start by hiding in the nearest cupboard.'

'I said I did that because I heard voices.'

'Well, so did Joan of Arc, but she didn't hide in cupboards.'

'And I thought it was burglars and I was going to spring out at them.'

'You told her that?'

'Yes.'

'It didn't strike you as a bit thin?'

'It was the best I could do. You must bear in mind that I had just been hit on the head by what felt like the Statue of Liberty. My mental processes were somewhat disordered.'

'How did she take it?'

'A little dubiously, it seemed to me. I suppose she assumed that I was loony.'

It was as if he had given her the cue for which she had been waiting. Her manner, hitherto that of Florence Nightingale condoling with a wounded soldier, took on the austerity of a governess who has discovered one of her charges in the act of raiding the jam cupboard. He had opened up a subject on which she had been brooding for some time.

'Which you are, of course,' she said tartly.

'I don't know what you mean.'

'Yes, you do. All that applesauce about loving that girl, and not being able to tell her so because she's rich and you aren't.'

'Oh, that?'

'Yes, that.'

'I can't help the way I feel, can I?'

'Of course you can. It only needs will-power.'

'Wouldn't she think I was just after her money?'

'Of course she wouldn't.'

'Everybody else would.'

'Well, what do you care about everybody else? Let

126

'em eat cake. What does it matter if a lot of fatheads think you're on the make? And in passing why don't you give a thought to the poor girl?'

'You mean the rich girl.'

'Well, whatever she is, why don't you take her agony into your calculations?'

'Her what?'

'Agony was what I said. Distress, misery and torment, if you prefer it. Or anguish.'

She had opened up a new line of thought, one which had not occurred to Jerry. A modest young man, it had never struck him before that he was a sort of demon lover for whom women wailed. He stared at her, aghast.

'Do you really think she feels like that?'

'Of course she does. There she is, unfortunate little rat, yearning for you, pining for you, looking on you as her official Prince Charming, saying to herself every morning "Perhaps today he will come riding up on his white horse and put his arms round me and tells me he loves me", and what happens? Not a yip out of you. I should imagine she would be in a horrible state, crying buckets, refusing nourishment, reducing herself to skin and bone and biting large holes in her pillow every night.'

She had made her point. Just as she had convinced him when using her eloquence on behalf of the Lincolnshire and Eastern Counties Glass Bottling Corporation, she convinced him now. How right she was, he felt, in saying that he ought to be certified. Any man who could behave as he had been behaving—to all intents and purposes like that base Indian who was such a poor judge of jewellery—could step straight into the most exclusive lunatic asylum and they would show him off to visitors as their star exhibit.

His scruples, of which he had been so proud, had gone with the wind. He advanced on her and breathed her name passionately.

'Jane! ... Jane, will you—'

'Half a mo', cocky.'

It was not she who had spoken. Seeming to have popped up out of a trap, Chippendale had joined them.

'Sorry to intrude, chum,' said Chippendale with a courteous wink, 'but the boss would like a word with you.'

2

Although it had been said of Crispin Scrope with considerable justice that if men were dominoes, he would be the double blank, he was not without a certain intelligence and the ability to deduce and draw conclusions. Informed that his nephew Gerald had been found crouched in a cupboard in Mrs. Bernadette Clayborne's bedroom, it had occurred to him almost immediately that he must have had some reason for being there. Nephews, he told himself, do not crouch in cupboards merely to satisfy an idle whim, and a few moments intensive thought had brought the solution of the mystery. He had written to Willoughby to tell him to disregard their telephone conversation, for since then he had changed his mind and was now heart and soul in favour of de-miniature-izing Mrs. Clayborne, but Willoughby, feeling in his practical way that two heads were better than one, must have added Gerald to his corps of minions. It was only what might have been expected of a man so eager to get results.

Hope, crushed to earth by Chippendale's withdrawal from the hunt, began to stir once more. Gerald had failed as a searcher of rooms, but he was a bright young fellow and might have other ideas, and ideas were what were particularly needed, for he himself had none.

Wasting no time on arguments and pleadings with Chippendale, for Barney's prowess with statuettes had plainly impressed him so deeply that he could see they would be futile, he said:

'Do you know where Mr. West is?'

'Probably putting his head under the tap some-where.'

'Find him and tell him to come and see me imme-diately,' said Crispin, and disdained to answer Chippen-dale's enquiry as to whether it was his intention to kiss the place and make it well.

Jerry's mood as he entered was not sunny. That of a man who has sustained a head wound and has sub-sequently been interrupted in a proposal of marriage seldom is. He eyed Crispin bleakly and shot out a surly 'Yes?'

Crispin did not fail to notice the absence of bonhomie, and bearing in mind the urgency of conciliating his only ally he set himself to supply bonhomie enough for two.

'Sit down, Gerald. Will you have a cigar, Gerald?'

'No, thanks.'

'A drink?'

'No, thanks,' said Jerry.

His manner was damping, but Crispin persevered.

'I asked you to come here, Gerald, because I have something to discuss with you.'

'Oh?'

'Yes, something very important. Chippendale has been telling me of your unpleasant encounter with Mrs. Clayborne.'

'Oh?'

'I hope your head is less painful?'

'It isn't.'

'Still aching?'

'More than ever.'

'I am sorry. A nasty thing to have happened. Mrs. Clayborne is very robust. She found you in her cup-board, I understand. You were looking for your Uncle Willoughby's miniature, of course?'

Jerry's mood of resentment changed to one of

bewilderment. His estimate of Crispin's intelligence had always been more or less identical with that of the critic with the dominoes metaphor. Certainly he had never credited him with clairvoyance.

'I should mention,' Crispin continued as he stared dumbly, 'that Willoughby rang me up on the telephone informing me of the theft of the miniature and urging me to do everything in my power to recover it. He wanted me to search Mrs. Clayborne's suite. I was somewhat taken aback, but naturally I wished to do what I could to help him, so I confided in Chippendale and promised him a substantial emolument if he would undertake what you might describe as the active work.'

'So that was why Chippendale was there!'

'Exactly. He was searching. He is an experienced searcher. As a boy, when his father won money at the dog races and hid it to prevent his mother finding it, he used to track it down on his mother's behalf, and always, I understand, successfully. I gather that it is a gift, and I was relying on him absolutely, but being an eyewitness of your encounter with Mrs. Clayborne has unfortunately had a lowering effect on his morale. He has just told me that he wishes to have nothing further to do with a woman of such direct methods. His actual expression was a woman with such a wallop.'

'He's including himself out?'

'Precisely.'

'And you want me to take up the torch from where he has dropped it?'

'You put it poetically but accurately.'

It seemed to Jerry that before anything in the nature of a partnership could be formed a strict understanding must be arrived at. There were limits to what he was prepared to do to oblige his Uncle Bill, even though success would mean so much to himself. Nor could such an attitude be considered unreasonable. If Barney's direct methods had had such a pronounced effect on

Chippendale, a mere onlooker, it is not surprising that the actual recipient of her attentions should hesitate to come within arm's reach of her again.

'You aren't expecting me to play a return date in her suite, are you?' he said. 'Because if so...'

'No, no,' said Crispin, though that was what he had been hoping for. 'Once bitten, twice shy.'

'And the burned child dreads the fire.'

'Precisely. Though if some afternoon I were to take her for a long country walk?'

'Not even then.'

'Or to Salisbury to see the cathedral?'

'The car would break down before it got out of the gates, and she would be back, complete with statuette.'

'And she has already seen the cathedral. No, we must hit on something else. Let us think.'

They thought.

'Have you any ideas?' asked Crispin after a pause.

'One.'

'I have, too.'

'Two?'

'I am sorry. I should have said "also". I should be glad to hear yours.'

'It's just a suggestion.'

'Quite. Proceed.'

'Well, I remembered a detective story I read as a kid. There was a kleptomaniac who was always pinching things from people, and one day he took a packet of bank notes from the overcoat pocket of a man named Gibbs. He was dining with Gibbs and the coat was hanging in the hall and Gibbs had forgotten to take the stuff out, and the fellow got away with it.'

'Interesting. But how does it help us?'

'I'm coming to that. The detective called on the fellow and said, "Could you let me have the package you took from Mr. Gibbs's overcoat pocket on the night of January the twenty-third?", and the fellow said, "He wishes it returned, does he?" and handed it over.'

There was a somewhat lengthy silence. Watching Crispin fingering his moustache, Jerry had the uneasy feeling that he had not been as bright as he could have wished. It was a long time since he had read the story he had mentioned, and he rather fancied he had left something out.

'H'm,' said Crispin.

'You don't think much of it?'

'Not a great deal. The kleptomaniac seems to have been of a singularly easygoing disposition. I doubt if Mrs. Clayborne would prove so amenable.'

'Perhaps you're right. Yes, I suppose she would be more likely to bean you with the nearest statuette.'

'Me?'

'I was assuming that you, as an older man whose personality carries more weight, would undertake the negotiations.'

'You were mistaken,' said Crispin.

There was another silence. Jerry resumed the conversation.

'You said you had an idea.'

'Ah yes. Mine oddly enough also derives from a detective story. You are familiar with the exploits of Sherlock Holmes?'

'Know them by heart, but which of them would be any use to us? Would it be the *Adventure of the Five Orange Pips*? Are you planning to intimidate Mrs. Clayborne by sending her five orange pips, with a message telling her to put the miniature on the sun dial?'

'That had not occurred to me.'

'It might work. It would depend, of course, on whether she's allergic to orange pips. Many people aren't.'

'My plan is based not so much on a story as on something Holmes said in one of the stories. He said, if you recall, that when a house is on fire, everyone's impulse is to carry out from the flames the thing most precious to them; in Mrs. Clayborne's case, I think we may assume, the miniature. That seems to me a correct statement of human psychology.'

Jerry, having no moustache to finger, fingered his chin.

'Let's get this straight. For the moment I'm a little fogged. Are you proposing to set fire to Mellingham Hall?'

Crispin could not repress a wistful sigh. The picture of a heavily insured Mellingham Hall in flames was a very attractive one.

'That will not be necessary. You will simply ring the fire alarm.'

'*I* will?'

'It is young man's work.'

'I don't know where the fire alarm is.'

'I can show you.'

'I just press a button, do I?'

'You pull a rope. This rings a bell.'

'And out will pop Mrs. Clayborne?'

'I think we can rely on that.'

'With the miniature on her?'

'Presumably.'

'How does one find out? Does one frisk her?'

'I beg your pardon?'

'Do I pass my hands up and down her person, as in the movies?'

'I never thought of that.'

'And if she has got the thing on her, do I knock her down and grab *it*?'

'I did not think of that, either. No, I am afraid my suggestion does not prove to be very fruitful.'

'I wouldn't call it frightfully hot.'

'It's just as good as yours,' said Crispin with spirit.

'Just about,' Jerry had to agree. 'You haven't anything better?'

'I am afraid not.'

'Nor have I. The fact is it's impossible to get one's brain working properly in a stuffy library full of volumes of collected sermons. I can only think when I'm walking. I shall now put in four or five miles, and I hope when I get back to have something sizzling to submit to you.'

When Jerry returned some eighty minutes later, his face was flushed not only with exercise but with the light of inspiration. He informed Crispin that he had got it.

'The test of a great general,' he said, 'is his ability to learn from his defeats. Where the second-rater on getting clobbered by the opposition merely says "Ouch!" and retires to his tent and tries to forget, the top-notcher lights his pipe and sits down and says to himself "That last battle was a bit of a wash-out and certainly won't look any too well in my Reminiscences, but what I have to do now is brood on it and see how I can profit by its lesson". Take me, for example. I have suffered a defeat. I have made myself an object of the deepest suspicion to Ma Clayborne, for I'm not ass enough to suppose that she swallowed that story I told her. She has me docketted as a bad guy who will bear watching, and she will believe anything anyone says to my discredit. So what you must tell her on her return from whooping it up at the vicarage is that I've been a sneak thief since boyhood and a constant grief and anxiety to the family. Say I was sacked from school for stealing, broke my mother's heart and have cost you a fortune in hush money. The only prudent thing for anyone to do who's staying at Mellingham while I am there you tell her, is to hand over anything they value to you and you'll put it in the safe, like when you go on and ocean liner and entrust your jewellery to the purser. Otherwise, you say, I shall infallibly get away with it. Are you prepared to bet that she won't thank you brokenly for tipping her off and give you the miniature?'

Crispin drew a deep breath.

'Gerald, this is genius!'

'I thought you'd be pleased.'

'I do not see how it can fail.'

'It can't. So off you go. She must be back by this time.'

3

Crispin went on his way with a buoyant stride far different from the shambling totter with which he had mounted the stairs so short a while ago, and Jerry sat thinking how extraordinarily lucky his uncles were to have someone as clever as himself to extricate them from their difficulties. No need for them to worry when on the horns of dilemmas, for there were few of these that would not yield to treatment by G. G. F. West. He wondered why a man so gifted had never thought of going into the diplomatic service.

He had been musing thus for some minutes, when the door opened and Chippendale entered with his customary affable air of being sure of his welcome. Jerry felt no surprise on seeing him. He had been at Mellingham long enough to know that, whatever other shortages might occur in that stately home of England, there would never be any stint of Chippendale's society. He had no wish, however, for a tête-à-tête with him.

'He isn't here,' he said, hoping to avert this.

'Pardon, cocky?'

'If you're looking for Mr. Scrope, he's stepped out.'

Chippendale disclaimed any desire to see Mr. Scrope. He had come, he said, to enquire after Jerry's head and to verify his suspicion that it's owner's sojourn in the cupboard had been linked up with the search for the ruddy miniature. Sifting the evidence, he said, he had deduced that Jerry must be one of Mr. Willoughby Scrope's corps of assistants.

'Like you,' said Jerry, seeing no point in not admitting the charge.

'Well, they always say The more, the merrier. I'm no longer an operative, by the way.'

'Yes, my uncle told me you had ratted.'

The verb appeared to pain Chippendale.

'I've handed in my resignation, yes. I thought it best when I saw what lengths that dame would go to when stirred. Which reminds me, how's your poor head?'

'Not too good.'

'I thought it wouldn't be. Muscular dame, that. Strong wrists. Not sure I altogether approve of her. I like women to be feminine. American, isn't she? I thought so. They get that way in America from going on all those demonstration marches and battling the police. And talking of police, do you know the thought that crossed my mind as I watched her start her backswing? I was wishing it could have been Simms in that cupboard instead of you.'

Jerry said he would have been glad if it had been anybody in the cupboard instead of him. Who, he asked, was Simms?

'The local Gestapo. Constable Simms he calls himself. Him and me have a feud on owing to his harsh and arbitrary methods.'

'Harsh, is he?'

'And arbitrary. If you described him as going about seeking whom he might devour, you wouldn't be far wrong.'

'Sounds a stinker.'

'And is. I'd like to get back at him, but it's difficult with a fellow that size.'

'I see what you mean. You would be giving away too much weight. He's a big stinker, and you're a little stinker.'

Again Chippendale showed in his manner that he found Jerry lacking in tact.

'Well, that's one way of putting it.'

'So you're baffled.'

'Yes and no. I wouldn't care to take on a human hippopotamus like him in physical combat, but I have a scheme or method as you might say which would lower his pride to the dust if put into operation. Only I'd need an accomplice.'

'Better advertise. What is the scheme or method?'

'I'll tell you. I must begin by saying that this bluebottle has trouble with his feet.'

But having begun by saying it he was precluded from elaborating his theme by the re-entry of Crispin, and Jerry was left to ponder, if he cared to do so, on what connection Constable Simms's foot trouble could have with the triumph Chippendale was hoping for, always provided that he could find the necessary accomplice. Possibly Simms suffered from corns, and it would be the task of the accomplice to tread on them. Though why this, though painful, should lower the officer's pride to the dust it was not easy to see.

As Crispin advanced into the room, it was plain that all was not well with him. He was wearing the unmistakable air of a man who has failed to find the blue bird. His eyes protruded, his moustache drooped, and what hair he had was ruffled as if he had been running agitated hands through it. He looked like one of those messengers in Greek tragedy who come bringing news of ruin and disaster, and they were about as glum a lot as you could meet in a month of Sundays.

But there was this difference between him and such a messenger. The latter would have made a long speech full of 'Woe, woe' and stuff about the anger of the gods. Crispin got down to the *res* without preamble.

'She's given that miniature to the vicar for his jumble sale in aid of the church lads annual outing,' he said, speaking in a voice which for its hollowness and lack of vivacity might have come from a tomb.

Chapter Thirteen

The shock of bad news affects different people in different ways. Some hardy souls are able to take it with a stiff upper lip, but on none of the three upper lips at the moment under advisement was there anything remotely resembling rigidity. Crispin, who on receipt of Barney's bombshell had quivered like a jelly in a high wind, was still quivering: Jerry uttered an odd gurgling sound which might have proceeded from the children's toy known as the dying rooster: while Chippendale once more requested some unspecified person to chase his Aunt Fanny up a gum tree. It would not be too much to say that consternation reigned.

Crispin was the first to break the silence which had fallen on the room.

'She must be mad! Why, the thing's a Gainsborough. It's worth a fortune. What on earth could have made her do it?'

'Religion, cocky,' said Chippendale, never at a loss for the logical explanation. 'Religious fervour. It takes the females that way sometimes. I had an aunt who pawned my father's false teeth in order to contribute to the mission for propagating the gospel among the unenlightened natives of West Africa. Grilled subsequently by the family, she said she was laying up treasure in heaven, but she can't have laid up much, because false teeth are what you might call a drag on the market and don't fetch more than a few bob. It's my Aunt Myrtle I'm speaking of,' he went on, as if anxious to obviate any chance of confusion between this relative and the one who was so often chased up gum trees. 'I'll tell you something funny about my Aunt Myrtle ... Pardon?' he said, for Jerry had spoken.

Jerry explained that he had merely said 'Damn your Aunt Myrtle', and Chippendale, amused by the coincidence, told him that those were the very words his father had uttered on becoming aware of his bereavement.

'He was greatly attached to those teeth. He used to be able to crack Brazil nuts with them, and of course without them he couldn't preserve that debonair appearance. You'd hardly believe the things he said about the unenlightened natives of West Africa, though a moment of reflection would have told him that they weren't to be blamed for what had occurred. But I merely brought up that about my Aunt Myrtle to illustrate what I was saying with ref to women coming over all religious.'

Jerry, who was recovering only slowly and had not yet regained his usual amiability, asked sourly what was so religious in giving a donation to a jumble sale in aid of the Church Lads Annual Outing.

'I don't even know what church lads are.'

Chippendale seemed surprised at this gap in a friend's knowledge. Always eager to be of help, he hastened to fill it.

'They're just a lot of piefaced young perishers who collect in gangs in these rural parishes. Choir boys, mostly. They attend Sunday school and sing in the choir, and once a year they let 'em loose to have an outing. They go off in a charabanc with buns and hardboiled eggs and lemonade, and that of course runs into money. You don't get buns and hardboiled eggs and lemonade for nothing, let alone hire of charabanc and tip to driver, so the vicar has this jumble sale to bump up the cash receipts. Ask me, he's a mug to take the trouble. Much simpler to drown the little barstards in a bucket. That would teach them to make personal remarks about people's physical appearance. Do you know what one of them called me yesterday?'

The question was addressed to Crispin, who responded with a petulance equal to Jerry's.

'I do not wish to hear what he called you yesterday.'

'I'd rather not have heard it myself. Where they pick up these expressions is more than I could tell you. In Sunday school, I suppose. But I was telling you about my Aunt Myrtle. She had false teeth same as father, but whereas his fitted him like the paper on the wall, hers didn't, and she had to get another set, which left her with the first lot on her hands. She never liked wasting anything, but she couldn't think what to do with them. Why she didn't pawn them and give the proceeds to the West Africans, I don't know, but apparently it didn't occur to her. The idea she got after a lot of thought was to make them the basis, if you know what the word means, of a mouse trap. She got a scientific feller she knew to fix one up with the teeth inside it in such a way that any mouse that shoved its nose in would get its loaf of bread snapped off, and all would have been well if she hadn't gone into the kitchen in the dark one night with no shoes on and tripped over the trap, which promptly came down like a ton of bricks on her big toe, nearly severing it. And the doctors at the hospital decided to amputate in case gangrene might set in. And as the teeth were legally hers, the result was that she became the only woman in East Dulwich, where she was living at the time, who could truthfully say that she had bitten her own toe off. It gave her prestige. Well, I can't stay chatting with you all day, mates, so if you don't want me for anything further, I'll be getting about my duties.'

After he had left them Jerry and Crispin sat in silence for perhaps an hour, full of what Alfred, Lord Tennyson, once described as thoughts too deep for tears. Of the two mourners it was Jerry who mourned the more bitterly, for he was tortured by the galling realization that in supposing that he had the sort of brain that can solve any dilemma he had been mistaken. As Chippendale would have said, it lowered his pride to the dust.

He could see no way out of the impasse. The idea of burgling the vicarage and tying the vicar up and sticking lighted matches between his toes till he disgorged the miniature he dismissed as impracticable. It had a momentary attraction, but prudence told him that that sort of thing would lead to his arrest by Constable Simms. And while this would probably result in the zealous officer being promoted to sergeant, he preferred that his rise to the heights should be achieved by other means. Let Constable Simms devote his energies to trying to alleviate the trouble he had with his feet, whatever that was.

As had happened before, he found the atmosphere of the library oppressive. It stifled his brain powers, such as they were. In the hope that fresh air and exercise would once again stimulate his little grey cells he rose and informed Crispin that he was going for a walk.

But before he could reach the door it opened, and he saw that Chippendale, the human homing pigeon, had returned.

2

He received chilly glances from both Jerry and Crispin. There are times when a nephew and uncle with a great deal on their minds are glad of the addition to their deliberations of a weedy little man who looks like a barnyard fowl, but this was not one of them.

What particularly irked them was the fact that this fowl impersonator was so plainly in the best of spirits, looking indeed as if he had just bought the world and paid cash down for it. That was what in their despondent mood they found so hard to bear. A melancholy Chippendale they could have endured: to a Chippendale in tears they might have extended a cordial welcome: but a Chippendale grinning all over his face in the manner popularized by Cheshire cats affected them like a knife stab in the breast, and they were about to clothe this sentiment in words, when the intruder spoke.

'Got a bit of good news for you, mates,' he said, and the bizarre idea that in the world as at present constituted there could be such a thing as good news held them speechless. Parted lips and bulging eyes showed how keen was their interest, but no verbal comment emerged. Except for a difference in clothes they might have been a couple of Trappist monks listening to a playlet of suspense on the radio.

Unlike Crispin, who, it will be remembered, had come to the point without delay, Chippendale preferred the circuitous approach. For a considerable time he might have been delivering an address to an audience of teenagers on the subject of how they should comport themselves when they went out into the great world. Have courage, he said. Never give up, he said. Tell yourself that it is darkest before the dawn and that though the storm clouds may lower, the sun will eventually come smiling through, he said.

But, he added, courage by itself was not enough. It was also essential to have the ability to think quick. If you couldn't think quick when disaster was doing its stuff, you were sunk. He himself had always been a quick thinker, and in this matter of the ruddy vicar having got hold of the ruddy miniature he had spotted the course to pursue. And what was that? 'I'll tell you, chums,' said Chippendale, humanely putting them out of their suspense. 'We all want the ruddy miniature, don't we. Well, I've just been to the ruddy vicar and got it.'

He paused and seemed to be waiting for comment,

but his audience appeared unable to take in what he had said.

'Got it?' said Jerry.

'But how is that possible?' said Crispin.

'Everything's possible, cocky, if you think quick enough.'

'You mean the miniature is in your possession?'

'I'm glad you asked me that,' said Chippendale. 'Yes, my ruddy possession is just what it's ruddy well in.'

They had assimilated it now, and sharp cries, two in number, burst from their lips simultaneously. They gazed at him adoringly. There was no longer anything in their aspect to suggest that they held the view that with the possible exception of animalculae in stagnant ponds he was the lowest form of life which civilization had yet produced.

Neither was slow with his applause. Jerry said Chippendale was a marvel. Crispin endorsed this opinion. A superman, Jerry said, and Crispin said that that was just the word he had been groping for. He added that he found it difficult to understand how even one so gifted could have achieved such a triumph.

'How did you manage it?' said Jerry.

'I went to him and pitched the tale.'

'How do you mean?'

'Yes,' said Crispin. 'What tale did you—ah—pitch?'

'Give you three guesses.'

'Please!'

'Well, all right,' said Chippendale, relenting. 'I told him the girl in the picture was the dead spit of a girl I'd loved and lost owing to her having died in my arms of what's the ailment beginning with an l, not leprosy, starts with a leuk.'

'Leukaemia?'

'That was it. I said she had kicked the bucket from an attack of leukaemia and I wanted the thing to remind me of her, so would he be so kind as to allow me to buy it before the sale opened and the general purchasing public was let in. I said it meant everything to me and I was sure he would understand, and he said Yes, yes, in a very real sense he understood and certainly certainly he would cough it up. So he did, and I came away with it, wrapped up in a bit of brown paper. Simple.'

'Admirable,' said Crispin, correcting his choice of adjectives. 'I cannot praise your ingenuity too highly.'

'Nor me,' said Jerry. 'It just shows . . .'

He paused, and Chippendale asked what it just showed.

'How right you were about the sun coming smiling through,' said Jerry. He had been about to say that it just showed that you can't judge a man's brain power by his looks, because even one who closely resembles the more unpleasant type of barnyard fowl in appearance can nevertheless possess the mental qualities of a great general, but he reflected in time that this might give offence. 'What have you done with the thing?'

'I've got it stowed away. I suppose I'd better give it to Mr. Scrope to take care of.'

Crispin agreed that that would be best, and Chippendale said he would attend to it in due course.

'But first there's one little matter I'd like disposed of. I wonder,' he said, addressing Jerry, 'if you remember me telling you that Constable Simms has trouble with his feet?'

Jerry assured him that he had not forgotten. He had been at something of a loss, he said, to see how the officer's misfortune, though of medical interest, fitted in with the scheme of things. The information, he thought, could more appropriately have been confided to a professional chiropodist than to himself.

'What's wrong with his feet?'

'During the morning and early afternoon,' said Chippendale, 'nothing, but towards evening, when he's done his rounds, they become heated, and this occasions him considerable discomfort. He didn't tell me so himself, him and me not being on those terms, but I had it from the wife of the postman, where he lodges. He told her, and she told me, that when he's come to the end of the long long trail, as the song says, his plates of meat felt as if they was on fire.'

'Too bad.'

'Depends on how you look at it. I regard it as a bit of luck. Manna in the wilderness, as you might say.'

'Why does it strike you like that?'

'Well, figure it out for yourself. What's the first thing a feller does when his plates of meat are feeling as if they were on fire? He shoves them in cold water.'

Jerry conceded this. So did Crispin. But they said they still could not see why this should be supposed to be of interest to two men who were in no sense intimates of Constable Simms.

'Scarcely know him by sight,' said Jerry. 'What have his incandescent plates of meat got to do with us?'

'You'll find out all in good time,' said Chippendale. He spoke with the quiet patience of a teacher in an elementary school who is having a difficulty in explaining something obvious to two pupils who are slow in the uptake but is determined to drive it into their thick heads. 'Do you know the brook?'

Crispin continued fogged. He said he had a friend of that name, but had not seen him for years.

'The brook that runs into the lake,' said Chippendale, losing his patience a little.

'Yes, yes, of course I know that brook.'

'Well, after he's done his last round, Simms goes and takes off his boots and sits beside it and lets the water run over his feet.'

'His plates of meat, you mean,' said Jerry.

'It's the same thing,' said Chippendale, now openly impatient. 'One drops into this habit of talking rhyming slang. The point I'm trying to establish is that Constable

Simms sits there dabbling his extremities in the brook.'

'So what?'

'So anybody who wanted to could creep up behind him and give him a push and immerse him.'

Jerry had no difficulty in following what was in his mind. He remembered what the speaker had said about lowering Constable Simms's pride to the dust. Such an immersion would undoubtedly go far towards accomplishing this. Once again he was compelled to admire the man's grasp of strategy and tactics.

'When are you going to do it?' he asked almost with reverence.

The question plainly surprised Chippendale.

'Who, me?' he said. 'I'm not going to do it. Why, lord love a duck, I'd be the prime suspect, my relations with the son of a what-not being so strained, and if I hadn't an unbreakable alibi I'd be for it. It's a job for one of you two. You'd better toss for it.'

This seemed reasonable to Jerry. He, Crispin and Chippendale were allies, as closely linked together as those boys of the Old Brigade who stood steadily shoulder to shoulder, and he did not consider that it was asking too much of an ally to suggest that he should push a policeman into a brook. It was just one of those trifling good turns which allies are entitled to expect of one another. If one of the three Musketeers had asked the other two Musketeers to push Cardinal Richelieu into the Seine, the other two Musketeers would have sprung to the task with their hair in a braid.

Looking at Crispin and hoping from him a similar endorsement of the plan, he was astonished to read in his face an unmistakable reluctance to co-operate. It would not be putting it too strongly to say that Crispin was aghast. When he spoke, his utterance, though only a monosyllable, showed this.

'What!'

'You heard, cocky.'

'I would not dream of doing such a thing.'

'Well, you'd better start dreaming, or you won't get that miniature. I'll take it up to London myself and collect the whole two hundred your brother Bill is offering for it. Treat me right, and you'll have your cut. Refuse to do the simplest little thing I ask you to, and not a penny do you get. So let's hear from you, chum.'

Jerry added his weight to the Chippendale cause.

'I think you'd better, Uncle Crispin.'

'You bet he'd better.'

'You might win the toss.'

'Of course he might.'

'And even if you don't win, what's there to worry about? The thing'll only take you a minute. Just one good shove.'

'Easy as dipping a bit of bread into your gravy.'

'And if he catches you, you can say you were merely giving him a friendly pat on the back and your hand slipped.'

To say that these arguments, sound though they were, convinced Crispin would be an exaggeration. He continued to feel as if he were playing a stellar role in a particularly unpleasant nightmare. But Chippendale's frank statement of what he intended to do if his wishes were not respected carried more weight than the natural reluctance to treat an officer of the law as a bit of bread.

'Very well,' he said in a low, husky voice.

'That's the spirit,' said Jerry, and Chippendale, all sunshine again, agreed that that was the spirit.

'Then away we go,' he said. 'I'll flip, and you call.'

He flipped.

'Heads,' muttered Crispin.

'And tails it is,' said Chippendale.

'Tough luck,' said Jerry. 'Well, I think what I had better do is nip up to London and acquaint Uncle Bill with the latest developments. He ought to find them not without a certain interest.'

He left with the object of looking up trains. Chippendale remained to give that word of advice which is so essential to a novice in the art of pushing policemen into brooks.

'Did you ever read those stories about a Red Indian chief called Ching something?' said Chippendale. 'I forget his name, but the thing I remember about him is that he never let a twig snap beneath his feet, and that's what I strongly advise you to do. Don't go saying to yourself that anyone as fatheaded as Simms is bound to be hard of hearing, because I happen to know he's not. Only the other day when he was throwing his weight about at the Goose and Gander I alluded to him, speaking to a friend in a quiet undertone, as an overbearing piece of cheese, and he overheard and made quite a thing of it. He'll be right on the key veeve if you start snapping twigs, so watch your step. Chingachgook, that was the name of that Indian chief, though I admit it doesn't seem likely. Well, I ask you. Imagine if you were having your baby christened at the church here and when the vicar said "Name this child" you said "Chingachgook". He'd send for Constable Simms and have you run in for drunk and disorderly. And now we've got back to the subject of Simms, bear in mind that he tips the scale at about sixteen stone, so you'll have to give him a good hard push. Get every ounce of weight and muscle into it.'

And with a cheery 'Chingachgook' Chippendale went on his way, leaving Crispin to his thoughts.

3

Barney, returning from tea at the vicarage, was not in her customary lighthearted mood. The vicar had done her well, denying her nothing in the way of buttered toast and cake, but in spite of this she could not help feeling depressed. She was thinking of G. G. F. West and his odd method of passing summer afternoons.

This was her first visit to England, and of course for all she knew it might be the normal practise of young Englishmen to hide in cupboards, possibly with the idea of jumping out and saying 'Boo!', but something seemed to tell her that this was an individual case and not just a sample of what was going on all the time all over the country. And this being so, it was difficult not to question Jerry's sanity. All the evidence appeared to point to his being as nutty as a fruit cake, which saddened her a good deal, for in the brief period in which they had been acquainted she had come to regard him with no little affection. A charming young man, she had told herself. A thousand pities that he should have this one weakness.

The more charitable theory that his activities might be a form of English humour had just presented itself, when her thoughts were diverted by the sight of Crispin. He came out of the house and started to walk in the direction of the lake. She hailed him, and he turned, and as he drew near the look on his face brought all the maternal instinct in her to life. It was the face of a man so weighed down with weight of woe that one wondered how he could navigate. His aspect reminded her of her husband on mornings of bygone January the firsts, when the late Mr. Clayborne owing to his habit of seeing the new year in had never been at his most robust.

'Crips!' she cried. 'Heavens to Betsy! You look like one of those bodies-which-have-been-in-the-water-several-days.'

And indeed there was a certain resemblance between Crispin and such a cadaver, for the passage of time had done nothing to diminish the horror of the task that lay before him. He was also experiencing pangs of remorse for the past. 'Oh, what a tangled web we weave,' he was saying to himself, 'when we touch a brother for two hundred and three pounds six and fourpence and then go and lose a hundred of it on a horse that comes in second.' Half the misery in life, he was thinking, is caused by horses that come in second; the other half by calling Heads when you might have known it was going to come down Tails.

A man cannot muse along these lines for any length of time without it showing in his appearance. All the concern which Barney had been feeling for an eccentric G. G. F. West was transferred to this new claimant for her commiseration. Nor is this to be wondered at. G. G. F. West was after all a mere acquaintance, but Crispin Scrope had become very dear to her. And he was so helpless, so vulnerable, so essentially the sort of man who without a woman's hand to guide him must inevitably trip over his feet and plunge into one of life's numerous morasses. Her heart ached for him.

'What is it, Crips? What's biting you?'

It was not an easy query for Crispin to answer. He was, as has been shown, far from being an intelligent man, but he was intelligent enough to realize that it would be injudicious to make any reference to the miniature. And yet everything urged him to confide in this angel of sympathy. He wanted to cleanse his stuffed bosom of the perilous stuff that weighs upon the heart, as Shakespeare would have put it.

A moment later he had seen the way. It involved falsifying the facts, but there are times when facts have to be falsified. Diplomats are doing it every day without their sleep. He decided to tell all—or a slightly edited version of all.

'It's Chippendale,' he said. 'He's blackmailing me.'

'Speak more clearly, Crips. It sounded just as if you were saying Chippendale was blackmailing you.'

'I did.'

'For heaven's sake! You been going in for crime of some sort?'

'No, no, of course not. But he says if I don't do what he wants, he'll tell the paying guests that he's a broker's man.'

'That would be bad?'

'Fatal. They'd all leave.'

'I thought you didn't like the paying guests.'

'I need their money.'

'Is that what Chippendale is after, money?'

'No, he wants me to push Constable Simms into the brook.'

A frown marred the smoothness of Barney's brow. Unlike Vera Upshaw, she never worried about getting wrinkles. When she suspected that she was being trifled with, she let nature take its course.

'Are you pulling my leg, Crips?' she said severely.

'No, no.'

'It sounds like it. Pushing Constable Simms into the brook, it doesn't make sense. Where's the percentage for Chippendale in that?'

Having successfully passed the point in his narrative where invention had had to take the place of truth, Crispin was now able to become fluent. In a shaking voice but with no pauses or hesitations he reminded her of the bad feeling which existed between Constable Simms and Chippendale, of the latter's expressed desire to make the former wish he had never been born, and of the difficulty a man weighing a hundred and twenty pounds always has in getting one weighing two hundred and ten into this frame of mind. He went on to emphasize the trouble the constable had with his feet and his habit of cooling them off in the waters of the brook.

'He sits on the bank and dabbles them, so it would be easy to push him in.'

'Easy as pie.'

'Only—'

'Only you have qualms about doing it.'

Crispin said that that was just it, and Barney said she quite understood.

'Doesn't do for a man in your position, that sort of thing. Didn't you tell me you were a judge or a magistrate or something?'

'I am a justice of the peace.'

'That makes it awkward. If he catches you, you'll come up before yourself and have to send yourself to the cooler for ninety days, coupled with some strong remarks from the bench. H'm. Not so good. But I see a way out.'

'You do?'

'Sure. I'll take on the job. Much better that way. Much more likely to get results. You're kind of frail, you mightn't push hard enough, but I'm the muscular type and if I lean on someone who's sitting on a bank and dabbling his feet in a brook, he goes into that brook special delivery. I'm glad that's settled. Takes a weight off your mind, I shouldn't wonder.'

And as she spoke these words love came to Crispin Scrope. It had come to him twice before in his earlier days and had flickered out, which was what had led to his two breach of promise cases, but this time he knew that it had come to stay.

4

Finding as the result of his researches in the Railway Guide that the last train to London had left some twenty minutes previously and was now well out of reach, Jerry returned to the library, feeling that with the girl he loved away he might as well be there as anywhere.

His mood was buoyant. Any doubts he may have had that he would soon be getting his money and so would be in a position to combine a proposal of marriage with self-respect had vanished. He had no high opinion of his Uncle Crispin's executive abilities, but surely even he was capable of pushing a policeman into a brook. And the policeman once pushed, the last obstacle to the happy ending would be removed.

These reflections, assisted by one of Crispin's excellent cigars, had the effect of inducing in him a sort of soppy benevolence towards the whole human race. When the door opened and Homer Pyle entered, he welcomed him with a bright smile. His acquaintance with him had been limited to a few exchanges on the subject of the weather, but he was a member of the human race and as such entitled to be smiled brightly at. In his present euphoric frame of mind he would have smiled brightly at Chippendale.

Knowing how interested Homer was in the weather, he made it the subject of his opening remark.

'Oh, hullo,' he said. 'Nice afternoon.'

'Yes,' said Homer.

'The sunshine. Good for the crops.'

'Yes,' said Homer.

'Going to hold up, apparently. They tell me there is a ridge of high pressure extending over the greater part of the United Kingdom south of the Shetland Isles. Sounds promising.'

'Yes,' said Homer. 'I am looking for Mr. Scrope.'

'He went out for a stroll. He should be back soon. Was it something important?'

'Very. There is a mouse in my bedroom. I want to draw it to his attention.'

Jerry was conscious of a feeling of pity for his Uncle Crispin. The paying guests, he supposed, were always coming to him and beefing about something. If it wasn't mice, it was dripping taps, and if it wasn't dripping taps, it was funny smells. Very wearing. No wonder the poor blighter had that careworn look.

'I'm sorry,' he said. 'No joke having a mouse in your bedroom.'

'It makes a scratching noise.'

'I'll bet it does. And you never know it won't go further and bite your toes. Well, I'll mention it to my uncle if I see him before you do, and I'm sure he'll lay on a cat.'

'If you will. Thank you.'

'Not at all.'

Homer withdrew, and Jerry was glad to see him go. At any other time he would have welcomed his company, for he was sure that, if drawn out, he would have a lot more interesting stuff to say about mice and bedrooms, a subject on which so far he had merely touched, but he wanted to be alone, to think of Jane.

He rose and began to pace the floor. This took him to the window, and he stood there looking out.

He was thus in a position to see the car which had just driven up to the front door. It was an expensive-looking car. One got the impression that it must belong to somebody who had no need to watch the pennies.

And so it did. The expensive-looking chauffeur alighted and opened the door, and Willoughby Scrope stepped out.

5

Jerry gave him a welcoming 'Hi!', adding perhaps unnecessarily 'I'm up here'. He was glad to see his Uncle Bill, for his advent had saved him a tedious journey to London. No need now to go to Chelsea Square and make his report. It could be done more comfortably on the premises of Mellingham Hall over a cigar and a drink. He pressed the bell for Chippendale, who entered just as Willoughby was settling himself in an arm chair.

'Want something, mate?' said Chippendale.

'Scotch and soda,' said Jerry, knowing his uncle's

tastes, and Chippendale in his affable way said, 'Scotch and soda, mate. Coming right up,' and withdrew. Willoughby followed him with an enquiring eye.

'Who's that?'

'Chippendale, Uncle Crispin's butler.'

'He doesn't look like a butler to me.'

'I said in my letter, if you remember, that he was a bit unusual.'

'Where on earth did Crispin dig him up?'

'I couldn't tell you.'

'He looks like a consumptive hen.'

'There is a certain resemblance.'

'Does he always call you mate?'

'Not invariably. Sometimes chum or pal or cocky.'

'If he addresses me like that I'll punch him in the eye.'

'I've often felt like doing it myself. But you've got to bear in mind one thing about Chippendale. He has a great brain. He thinks quick. Without him we should never have got your Girl In Blue back. Ah,' said Jerry, as the man they were discussing entered bearing a loaded tray. 'Put it down on that little table. Thank you, Chippendale.'

'The pleasure is mine, cocky,' said Chippendale courteously. 'You'll like this whisky, chum,' he added to Willoughby. 'It's good stuff. Not a headache in a hog's head.'

He withdrew again, pleased to have been of service, and Willoughby, though he had been addressed as chum, showed no disposition to speed him on his way with a punch in the eye. He was leaning forward in his chair, the whisky and soda temporarily forgotten, registering joy so competently that any motion picture magnate who had seen him would have signed him up on a long contract without hesitation.

'What did you say?' he gurgled. 'You've got it back?'

'All but.'

The reply appeared to displease Willoughby. He registered bewilderment and impatience.

'What the devil do you mean *all but*? Where is it?'

'Chippendale has it.'

'Chippendale? Why Chippendale?'

'It's rather a long story. Complex, too. I'd better tell it you from the beginning. You'll understand as the plot unfolds.'

Watching Willoughby's face as the plot did this, the motion picture magnate would have found his favourable opinion confirmed, for Willoughby, who had depicted joy, bewilderment and impatience so efficiently, now showed that he could do you horror, agony and dismay with equal facility.

'You mean,' he said, speaking hoarsely, like a Shakesperian actor with tonsilitis, 'that everything depends on Crispin pushing this policeman into a brook? Crispin couldn't push a Singer's midget into a brook. I wouldn't trust Crispin to squash a wasp with a teaspoon. Ring for this fellow Chippendale.'

'You want to speak to him?'

'I want to break his spine in three places if he doesn't hand over that miniature before I count ten.'

In Chippendale's demeanour, as he answered the summons, a physiognomist would have noted a certain deviation from the normal. As a rule he looked like a Wyandotte or Plymouth Rock with nothing particular to occupy its mind. Now, surprisingly, he was registering joy as wholeheartedly as Willoughby had done in his pre-horror and agony phase. Plainly something had occurred to bring the sun smiling through.

Willoughby, in whom years of financial solidity had developed a tendency towards imperiousness, seldom concealed his emotions. Possessing stocks and bonds in large numbers at his bank and money rolling in all the time, he did not have to. When he felt annoyed, he showed that he was annoyed. His manner in addressing Chippendale was curt.

'You!'

'Who me, cocky?'

'Yes, you, blister your blasted kidneys. Where's that miniature?'

'What miniature?'

It occurred to Jerry that the situation would be greatly clarified if introductions were performed.

'This is Mr. Willoughby Scrope, Chippendale.'

'Oh, *that's* who you are,' said Chippendale, relieved. 'I was hesitating to speak freely in front of you, because how was I to know that you were a bloke I could speak freely in front of? If you're the fellow who's the unseen mastermind behind our little group of workers, there's no need to seal my lips. Has Mr. West been telling you of all that's transpired?'

'Yes. Where's the miniature?'

'I'll be coming to that. Did he mention about the necessity arising for bunging the local police officer into the drink? Well, you'll be happy to hear that it's been attended to. I was looking out of the window just now, and I saw him squelching along soaked to the eyebrows. Not a dry stitch on him. It reminded me of that song about singing in the rain, not that he was singing, far from it. I've never seen a wetter copper except the time when one was trying to pinch my Uncle Reggie for street betting and my Aunt Myrtle threw a pail of soapy water over him, a wifely act for which she subsequently did thirty days without the option of a fine. So the thing that's been holding us up has been disposed of, and nothing stands in the way of me delivering the goods, which I shall be glad to do as soon as I can get to my room. The you-know-what is in the chest of drawers there, concealed beneath my socks and summer underwear. I'll go and get it.'

For some moments after Chippendale's departure Willoughby sat dumb and motionless, as if in a trance.

Then, reaching out for the whisky, he uttered a single word.

'Amazing!'

'That Chippendale's heart should have been so set on immersing Constable Simms?'

'No, that Crispin should have had the nerve and know-how to carry through such a delicate operation without a hitch. I wouldn't have thought he had it in him. What a lesson this should be to all of us never to write off a man as an incompetent poop simply because all his life he has behaved like an incompetent poop. Often he merely needs an incentive to bring out his hidden qualities. The crisis comes and his executive ability is revealed. He acts, as Crispin has done. It's really extraordinary. I could tell you stories of Crispin as a boy and in early manhood and for the matter of that even lately which would make you marvel that he ever escaped the loony bin. And yet in an enterprise which would have taxed the skill and ingenuity of an professional criminal ... Crips!' cried Willoughby, for the head of the family had tottered in and was gazing at the whisky decanter with the air of one who has come to journey's end. 'That gargoyle who calls himself a butler has just been telling us of your magnificent conduct.'

'Eh?' said Crispin. He seemed dazed.

'At the brook.'

'Oh, at the brook?' said Crispin.

'And I was saying to Jerry here that I never would have suspected you of such courage and adroitness. Didn't your nerve fail you for an instant?'

'No,' said Crispin. 'It had to be done, so I—er—did it. Any man would have done the same.'

'I disagree with you. It was—'

Willoughby was about to add the word 'heroic', but at this moment Homer Pyle entered the library. He had seen Crispin climbing the stairs and had followed him in order to fill him in on the subject of mice and bedrooms. He had got as far as 'Oh, Mr. Scrope, I am sorry to trouble you', when his eye fell on Willoughby.

'Why, Mr. Scrope,' he exclaimed. 'I did not know you were here.'

'Just arrived. I drove down. I had to see someone on business. Miss Hunnicut.'

'A charming young lady.'

'About a legacy she has had.'

'Ah yes, she was telling me about that only this morning.'

'I'll bet she didn't tell you all, because she wouldn't have known about the latest developments. But never mind that. How are you, Mr. Pyle?'

'In excellent health, thank you. I find the quiet of Mellingham soothing to the nerves.'

'Did you have a good time in Brussels?'

A shadow flitted over Homer's globular face, and for an instant he forgot mice and bedrooms. He was remembering dinners with Vera Upshaw, walks with Vera Upshaw and talks with Vera Upshaw when, if he had only been able to muster up courage, he might have asked her to be his.

'It was very educational,' he said. 'By the way, Mr. Scrope, you got my message?'

'Message?'

'I telephoned your office after you had left for your golfing holiday and told them to tell you that I had put your miniature in the middle drawer of your desk. I will explain in more detail when we are alone. For the moment I will merely say that I thought it safer,' said Homer significantly. 'I think you will understand what I mean. I was afraid that it might fall into the wrong hands if left on the mantelpiece. So after considerable reflection I came down at one o'clock in the morning—or it may have been nearer two—and transferred it to the middle drawer of the desk in your study.'

When he was strongly moved, as sometimes by the

vagaries of the office boy Percy, Willoughby's rather florid complexion always took on a deeper hue. It turned now to a royal purple, presenting a picture which would have interested a doctor in his blood pressure. His eyes bulged. He stared at Homer as a snail might have stared at another snail which had said something to shake it to its depths. His very ears had reddened, and it was evident from his manner that he was finding a difficulty in believing them.

'You mean ...' He choked. 'You mean it's been there all the time?'

'Exactly.'

'Then what's the one your sister gave the vicar?'

'I beg your pardon?'

'Mrs. Clayborne gave a miniature to the vicar for his jumble sale in aid of the church lads annual outing.'

'Oh, that one?' said Homer, and permitted himself a light laugh. 'She told me about that. She bought it for five shillings at a pawn shop and had intended to give it to you as a little token of her gratitude for your hospitality, but she felt that it was such an insignificant object that it was not worthy of inclusion in your collection. The reason I wished to see you, Mr. Scrope,' said Homer, changing the subject and addressing Crispin, 'is that there is a mouse in my bedroom. It comes out at night after I have gone to bed and makes a scratching noise which is very disturbing. But I see that you are occupied just now, so perhaps you will give me a few minutes later on.'

It was soon after he had left that Willoughby, who was still purple, was struck by a thought which did much to bring his complexion back to normal. Interrupting himself in the middle of a critique of Homer in which he stressed his disapproval of the latter's officiousness and practise of meddling in things that were no business of his, he said:

'Well, this saves me two hundred pounds,' and Crispin, grasping his meaning without difficulty, uttered a bleating cry which drew from his brother a sharp reproach.

'Don't make those animal noises, Crips. You surely aren't expecting me to pay out large sums of money for nothing.'

'But, Bill!'

'I pay by results. Business is business.'

Jerry put a question, on the answer to which much depended. His agitation, like Crispin's, was extreme.

'Does that apply to me, too?'

Willoughby considered the point, and relieved his mind.

'No, it's different with you. You'll get your money, and if you're going to marry Jane Hunnicut, you'll need it.'

'To preserve my self-respect, you mean?'

'Self-respect be blowed. You'll need it to pay the household bills.'

'I don't understand.'

'You will. By the way, where is she?'

'She went to London. She told me her New York lawyer had come over and wanted to see her.'

'I saw him this morning. Then he'll have told her.'

'Told her what?'

'That she hasn't a penny to bless herself with.'

'What!'

The ejaculation proceeded from both Jerry and Crispin simultaneously, Crispin's having the greater volume. His voice, as he went on speaking, had in it the suggestion of coming from a tomb which it had had when he was announcing Mrs. Bernadette Clayborne's donation to the vicar's jumble sale in aid of the church lads annual outing.

'You told me she was a millionairess and might buy the house.'

'Well, she isn't a millionairess and she won't buy the

house. I was exaggerating when I said she hadn't a penny, but she won't have much.'

'I think I'll go and lie down,' said Crispin.

The comparison, made earlier, between the younger of the brothers Scrope and a staring snail would have been equally applicable to Jerry as the door closed behind Crispin. His eyes bulged as Willoughby's had done, and he seemed to be experiencing the same difficulty in believing his ears.

'But what's happened? Have they found another will?'

'Hidden behind the third brick on the left in the kitchen wall? No, nothing like that. Jane Hunnicut gets everything, but the United States Federal sharks will see to it that that isn't much. The late Mr. Donahue appears to have been one of those men who don't approve of income tax. He hadn't paid his for fifteen years. You can imagine what the sharks will do with a case like that. They'll have a field day. Add debts, liabilities for surtax, capital gains tax, death duties and all the rest of it, and there won't be a lot left. The same thing happened with a client of mine the other day. His gross estate was four hundred thousand pounds, and they whittled it down to something like seven thousand net. If Jane Hunnicut gets away with about that, she'll be lucky.'

'How absolutely wonderful!' said Jerry. 'How simply topping!', and as he spoke Chippendale entered. He was carrying a small brown paper parcel.

Willoughby eyed him austerely.

'What do you want?'

The question amused Chippendale. He cackled like the fowl he so resembled.

'What do *I* want? It's what *you* want, cocky. If you've forgotten what you sent me to fetch from beneath my summer underwear, you ought to see your medical adviser. Here it is, mate, but before we go any further

I've been thinking it over and I've decided to make a slight adjustment in the matter of terms.'

'What are you talking about, you blot?'

'The arrangement was that you were to cough up two hundred in the event of success attending the enterprise. It's not enough. Considering all I've been through on your behalf, shut up in small rooms with man-eating tigers and straining my brain to the utmost, we'll make it three hundred.'

That pretty shade of purple had begun to creep once more into Willoughby's cheeks.

'Three hundred!'

'Nice round sum.'

Willoughby heaved himself to his feet, breathing stertorously. He laid a large hand on Chippendale's shoulder.

'Come here,' he said, and led him to the window. 'See that lake?'

Chippendale admitted to seeing the lake.

'Well, go and jump in it, curse you,' said Willoughby. 'And one more thing. Before doing so, be sure to tie a good heavy brick round your repulsive neck.'

6

Having suggested this course of action, Willoughby made for the door. But while plainly anxious to remove himself as soon as possible from the society of Chippendale, he paused for a moment to throw a word at Jerry.

'I'll give you a cheque tomorrow,' he said, and was gone.

Chippendale, though taken aback as most people are when told to jump into lakes, was able to deduce the reason for his brusqueness. He had always been a man who could put two and two together.

'I opened my mouth too wide,' he said regretfully. 'I

ought to have stuck to the original terms.'

'No, it wasn't that,' said Jerry. 'It wouldn't have made any difference, whatever you had asked for. It was the wrong miniature.'

'How do you mean, it was the wrong miniature? It looked all right to me.'

Jerry would have preferred not to linger and embark on long explanations, for Jane had said she would be returning in the evening and he wanted to be at the gate to welcome her, but it seemed unkind to leave his former ally in a state of mystification. Even when a partnership has been wound up the partners have obligations.

'What happened was this,' he said.

He narrated the story briefly but well, and when he had finished Chippendale said, 'Cor stone the crows', not mentioning which crows or who was to cast the first stone.

'Are you telling me all my labour and toil has been for nothing?'

'I'm afraid so.'

'He won't brass up?'

'No.'

Chippendale mixed himself a whisky and soda and stood brooding for a space. When he spoke, it was with the same regret in his voice.

'I ought to have had a written contract.'

'Yes.'

'Though I might get him on the verbal agreement. Ought I to sue?'

'Waste of money, don't you think?'

'Perhaps you're right. What did he mean by saying my repulsive neck?'

'He was very much moved. Spoke wildly.'

'All the same, I shouldn't wonder if it wasn't slander. I'll have to consult my solicitor. Only I heard someone say he's one.'

'He is.'

'Then it's no good. They all stick together. I'll have to let it go. You know,' said Chippendale, his grievances apparently forgotten and the sunny side of his nature coming uppermost, 'I can't help laughing when I think of us wearing ourselves to a shadow trying to get the ruddy miniature and all the time it was the ruddy wrong one. Strikes me as funny, that.'

Had someone told Jerry that the time would come when he would find himself thinking highly of Chippendale and regarding him with affection, he would have scouted the idea as too far-fetched for consideration; but as he heard these gallant words his heart warmed to him. If Chippendale couldn't help laughing when Fate deprived him of a large sum of money, it seemed to him to indicate a nobility of character that demanded respect. He stood revealed as the sort of man Rudyard Kipling wrote 'If' about.

'You take it very well,' he said admiringly. 'I don't think I would have been as cheerful if Uncle Bill hadn't given me my money.'

'Was that what he was talking about when he said he'd be giving you a cheque?'

'Yes.'

'Much?'

'Quite a lot.'

It was Chippendale's turn to admire.

'I wouldn't have thought he was a bloke who would touch easy. Did you hypnotize him?'

Jerry laughed.

'It wasn't a touch. My father left me a packet in trust, with Uncle Bill as a trustee. I couldn't get it without his consent. He's now consented.'

'And it's all yours?'

'Yes.'

'Then I take it we now go to the pub and you stand drinks?'

It was an attractive idea, but Jerry shook his head.

'I'd love to, but I have a very important appointment. I'll tell you what, suppose I give you five quid and you go and do the drinking for both of us.'

'Five quid!'

'I should have said ten. Will that be all right?'

Chippendale removed any doubts he may have had. He said it would be more than all right. In an impassioned speech of acceptance he described Jerry as one of Nature's noblemen.

How long his eulogy would have continued one cannot say, for it was interrupted at an early stage by the entrance of a girl in maid's costume.

'Mr. Chippendale, Mr. Scrope wants you in the study.'

'Any idea what for?'

'It's something to do with Mr. Simms.'

'I thought it might be.' Chippendale turned to Jerry. 'I may have to call on you as a witness, chum. Where'll you be?'

'Somewhere by the main gate.'

'Right. I probably won't need you, but it's as well to know.'

Chapter Fourteen

Barney, as she returned from the scene of her waterside activities, was filled with the glow which comes from work well done. If, mingled with a pardonable self-satisfaction, there was a pang of womanly pity for the victim of those activities, it was only slight, for a man, she reasoned, who joins the police force must be aware that he is going to get new experiences and that these cannot all be agreeable. And, after all, a wet constable can soon be converted into a dry constable. Time the great healer, she felt, would see to it that Officer Simms would ere long be himself again. It only needed some brisk work with bath towels.

For the most part it was on the intelligent workings of Providence that she mused. As a girl at a fashionable New York seminary it had often been a source of regret to her that she was not petite and slender like so many of her schoolmates, but now she realized that Providence in fashioning her on more substantial lines had known what it was about. Those fellow students might have looked like bantamweight fairy princesses, but would they have been able to push a two hundred pound constable into a brook? They would not have so much as stirred him from his base. It would have been as if a butterfly had alighted between his shoulder blades. But thanks to her impressive physique, when she herself had applied the pressure, he had flown through the air like something shot from a gun. There are compensations for being the large or king size.

The inner glow increased as her thoughts turned to Crispin. Attracted to him at their first meeting by the fact that he was so unlike her first husband, in the days that had passed she had found that affection turning to something deeper. What in the beginning had been a mere impulse to stroke his head had grown into a fixed determination to take him for better or for worse and spend the remainder of her life with him. England was full of people who would have ridiculed the possibility of anyone falling in love with Crispin Scrope, the firm that did the repairs about the place heading the list, but she had managed it.

She had reached the front door and was about to go in, when he came out. He had changed his mind about lying down, reflection telling him that if he did lie down he would merely toss and turn and heave and twitch, and there was nothing to be gained by behaving like a Welsh rarebit at the height of its fever.

For a moment, eager to impart the good news, she did not observe his tragic aspect. Then it impressed itself on her, and she gave a cry of dismay.

'Crips! What's the matter? What is it? What's wrong?'

To this Crispin replied succinctly, 'Everything. Let's walk,' he said, and they turned down the drive towards the main gate.

'Tell me,' she said.

'I'm in an awful fix,' said Crispin.

Her alert mind leaped to the obvious explanation.

'Money?'

'Yes.'

'A bill?'

'Yes.'

'How much?'

'A hundred pounds.'

'Is that all?' said Barney, relieved. In the income tax bracket to which she belonged a hundred pounds or its equivalent in dollars was something which fell into the category of small change. She suggested the easy way out of his difficulties. 'Let me be your banker.'

Crispin shook his head.

'No.'

'Why not?'

'I can't touch you.'

'Oh, come on.'

'It's wonderful of you to offer it, Barney, but no.'

'You would lend it to me if you had it and I needed it.'

'That's different.'

'Why?'

'It just is.'

Barney gave up the struggle.

'Oh, well,' she said resignedly, 'if the Scropes have their code, that's that. I wish my Uncle Sam was as pernicketty about accepting money from me as you are. I've been supporting him for years. Who do you owe this hundred to?'

'The repairs people.'

'Oh, Chippendale's buddies. But didn't you tell me your brother Bill had given you the money to pay them?'

It was not easy for Crispin to confess his folly, but it was unavoidable.

'I lost a hundred of it on a horse.'

'But I thought you never played the races.'

'I haven't done for ages, but you know how it is when you get a really big tip.'

'I gave you one, on Brotherly Love, and you wouldn't take it.'

Crispin choked.

'I did take it,' he mumbled, and Barney stared, bewildered.

'Let's get this straight,' she said. 'My head's feeling as if it had a hive of bees inside it. Are you telling me you changed your mind and took my advice?'

'Yes.'

'And had a hundred on Brotherly Love?'

'Yes, with Slingsby's. I've still got an account there.'

'Then what in the name of goodness is all the song and dance about? You've made over twelve hundred pounds.'

It seemed to Crispin that the hive of bees to which she had objected had transferred itself to his head. It was full of their buzzing. Her words came to him dimly.

'Brotherly Love started at a hundred to eight.'

'But ...'

'But ... But ... you told me it came in second.'

'And so it did. Don't you ever read the papers?'

'No.'

'Well, you ought to. It came in second, half a length behind Muscatel, and there was an objection. Boring or bumping or something. The big brass went into a huddle, examined the evidence, found that Muscatel had bored or bumped or whatever it was, slapped its jockey's wrist and told him to be more careful in future and gave the race to Brotherly Love. You'll be getting Slingsby's cheque tomorrow or the day after, I guess. Depends on when settling day is. Here, hold up.'

Crispin had not actually fainted, but he had come near enough to it to arouse Barney's motherly concern. She led him to a rustic bench beside the drive. There she adopted what was apparently her policy for dealing with all human ills, massaging the neck. She did it as thoroughly and as competently as at their first meeting, and after experiencing for awhile that old familiar illusion of having been caught in some sort of powerful machinery Crispin sat up, announcing that he was all right now.

Barney contested this statement.

'You think you are,' she said, 'but you never will be till you've got a wife to look after you and see that you don't get into trouble. I spoke to you about this the other day, if you remember. You'll agree that if there's trouble around, you're sure to get into it?'

Crispin found it impossible to deny this. From early manhood he and trouble had been inseparable companions.

'So you need a wife.'

'I do.'

'Try me,' said Barney.

2

The glow which had been warming Barney before Crispin's arrival became intensified on his departure. On her advice he had gone to his study to write a cheque for the repair people, and she had remained on the rustic bench, going over in her mind each little detail of that tender scene.

Seated thus, she had a good view of the main gate, and through it now entered her brother Homer, accompanied by a girl. This she realized, must be the Miss Vera Upshaw whom Crispin had told her he was expecting. Trains from London stopped on request at Mellingham Halt half a mile from the village, and Homer had presumably gone to meet her there.

Her interest was immediately excited. If Homer went to meet girls arriving by train, it meant something. She had always looked on him as the least active girl-meeter of her acquaintance. The eye she bent on Vera as the two drew near was a speculative eye, and what she saw convinced her of the significance of Homer's deviation from the normal. This was not just a girl, but one of such surpassing beauty that one blinked on beholding her; the sort of girl who makes strong men catch their breath and straighten their ties; a girl Sheiks of Araby would dash into tents after like seals in pursuit of slices of fish; the last kind of girl, in short, she decided instantly, whom her poor misguided brother ought to have got mixed up with. She managed to respond with her usual heartiness as Homer made the introductions, but she remained uneasy. She had no illusions regarding his physical attractiveness, and in Vera she saw—quite correctly—a girl who was planning to marry him for his money.

Rather a sombre girl, this Miss Upshaw, she thought. She gave the impression of smiling with difficulty, possibly for fear of getting wrinkles.

But it was not this that was causing Vera's moodiness. Once again she was brooding on the apparent impossibility of extracting words of love from Homer. On the walk to the Hall from Mellingham Halt he had spoken quite freely on a number of subjects. He had called her attention to the fineness of the evening, he had spoken of the P.E.N. festivities at Brussels, and he had left her in no doubt that what he was sharing his bedroom with was a mouse, harping on this latter topic at some length: but on wedding bells and bishops and assistant clergy he had not touched, and she had almost made up her mind that he never would.

True, they had yet to sample the shady nooks and secluded walks of which her mother had spoken, but she had begun to doubt it even these would be shady and secluded enough to produce results.

With Barney fearing the worst, Vera perplexed and baffled and Homer virtually a total loss, conversation could not proceed other than fitfully. When after the third silence Vera said she supposed she ought to be going in and introducing herself to Mr. Scrope, the suggestion was welcomed.

'I'll come with you,' said Barney.

'I, too,' said Homer. 'I have already spoken to him briefly about my mouse, but I should be glad to go into it in more depth.'

'There is a mouse in Mr. Pyle's bedroom,' Vera explained, speaking with the weariness of a girl who has heard all she requires about mice.

'There may be more than one,' said Homer.

'I wouldn't be surprised,' said Barney. 'Crips denies his guests nothing. All right, let's go. He's in his study.'

'I am not altogether satisfied,' said Homer, as they moved off, 'that it is not a rat.'

3

Crispin's study, in which so many generations of Scropes had written so many letters to *The Times*, was on the ground floor, a dark and depressing room rendered even darker and more depressing at the moment of Chippendale's entry by the presence of Constable Simms, who, sitting with folded arms in a chair by the desk, somehow contrived to give it the atmosphere of a magistrate's court. A sensitive man, finding himself there, would have felt that he would be lucky if he got away with a mere fine.

Chippendale, who was not sensitive, entered with a jaunty and elastic step. He was about to face serious charges, but the only thing that bothered him on such occasions was the question of whether they could be made to stick, and he knew that those confronting him now could not. To say that his conscience was clear would be inaccurate, for he did not have a conscience, but he had what was much better, an alibi which no prosecuting counsel could break.

'You wished to see me, sir,' he said, substituting, as was his laudable custom when company was present, the more formal style of address for his usual chum or mate. 'Good evening, Mr. Simms,' he added courteously. 'You've dried yourself, I see. The last time I saw you, you were all wet. Did you fall into the lake or something?'

His attitude could not have been more sympathetic,

but all it drew from the officer was a tightening of the lips and a hardening of eyes which even before he had spoken had been eyes of stone. It was left to Crispin to explain the situation.

'Simms fell into the brook,' he said, and Chippendale clicked his tongue, amazed and concerned.

'Touch of what's known as vertigo?' he hazarded.

'He says somebody pushed him.'

'Pushed him?' Chippendale echoed, frankly bewildered. 'What, *pushed* him? Who would have done a thing like that?'

'He accuses you.'

'And you'll get a stiff sentence,' said the constable, speaking with relish. 'Six months, I shouldn't wonder.'

Chippendale's manner took on a strange dignity. He drew himself to his full height, which even when full was not much, and stared defiantly. He did not actually say 'There is no terror, cocky, in your threats, for I am armed so strong in honesty that they pass by me like the idle wind which I respect not', but he made it evident that that was what he was thinking.

'I'm as innocent as the driven snow,' he said.

'Ho!'

'And I can prove it.'

'Ho!'

'When did this outrage occur?'

'As if you didn't know.'

The desk was handy for being struck with a clenched fist. Chippendale struck it.

'Answer my question!'

'Please answer his question, Simms.'

'About har-past five,' said the constable gruffly.

Chippendale would have struck the desk again, but he had hurt his hand the first time. He confined himself to a withering look.

'At half-past five,' he said, 'I was in the library in conference with Mr. Scrope and his nephew Mr. West.

174

I could call on Mr. West to vouch for the truth of my statement, but it won't be necessary. Mr. Scrope can do all the vouching that's required. That's so, isn't it, Mr. Scrope?'

'Perfectly correct,' said Crispin. 'At half-past five, Simms, Chippendale was with me and my nephew in the library.'

Constable Simms was plainly disconcerted, but England's police do not give in easily.

'Might have been earlier than har-past.'

Chippendale repeated the withering look.

'How much earlier?'

'Quarter of an hour, maybe.'

'So you say now that the outrage may have taken place at a quarter past five?'

'About then.'

'At a quarter past five,' said Crispin, 'Chippendale was already in the library.'

It was evidence against which the stoutest hearted could not contend. Constable Simms said 'HO', rose from his chair and made for the door.

'So now,' said Chippendale, 'you know the meaning of the words "innocent as the driven snow", and I think you would be well advised, cocky, not to go about making these wild accusations without a lot of evidence. Or tittle. Otherwise you'll be getting yourself into serious trouble. I may or may not see my solicitor about this, but if I don't, it'll only be because I've got a tender heart. The idea of thinking I'd do a thing like bunging you into a brook. Ask me, it was one of the church lads. Don't you agree, Mr. Scrope?'

Crispin said that it was certainly a tenable theory.

'If you will go sitting beside brooks in a locality congested with church lads, in my opinion you're just asking for it. One of them was bound to get ideas into his head. And you wouldn't have heard him creeping up behind you, because he wouldn't let a twig snap beneath his feet, like that fellow Chingachgook we were talking about the other day, Mr. Scrope. So if I were you, I'd make searching—'

He would have added the word 'enquiries', but the door had closed behind the constable. He turned to Crispin.

'We didn't half put it across that copper, did we, mate? What you'd call a famous victory, like in the poem. Ever read that poem? I learned it in Sunday School. Kid finds a skull and takes it to her grandfather, and he tells her about the battle they had in those parts, out in Belgium somewhere it was. I've forgotten most of it, but I remember it ended up "Things like that, you know, must be at every famous victory." '

'And one of the things that are going to be at this famous victory,' said Crispin with satisfaction, 'is that I shall be seeing the last of you, Chippéndale.'

'I don't get you, chum.'

'I am sending your employers a cheque for what I owe them.'

'You're paying them off?'

'I am.'

'Cor stone the crows, I never thought you'd make it. What did you do? Rob a bank?'

'I won twelve hundred pounds on a horse.'

'Cor chase—' Chippendale began, but before he could issue instructions concerning his Aunt Fanny and gum trees he was interrupted by the entry of Barney, Homer and Vera.

Barney opened the conversation.

'Hullo there, Crips. Not busy, are you?'

'No longer, madam,' Chippendale informed her in his genial way. 'The police have left.'

'Police? Has the joint been raided?'

'Ha ha, madam. No, merely a private personal matter. Somebody pushed Constable Simms into the the brook.'

'You astound me. Well, he had a fine day for it. This

is Miss Upshaw, Crips.'

'Pleased to meet you, miss,' said Chippendale. 'Well, if there's nothing further, Mr. Scrope, I'll be getting along. Mr. West—'

'Mr. West?' said Vera.

'My nephew Gerald,' said Crispin. 'Do you know him?'

'Quite well. Is he staying here?'

'Yes.'

'How delightful.'

'Nice fellow, Jerry West,' said Barney, and Chippendale was swift to endorse this opinion.

'The whitest man I know,' he said. 'He's just given me a substantial sum to drink his health.'

'Why did he do that?'

'Exuberance, madam. Gaiety of spirit. He's come into money. Something to do with the termination of some trust he was connected with. I didn't follow all the details, but the salient fact emerged that he is now in the chips. And good luck to him, say I. It couldn't have happened to a nicer bloke.'

It was possibly the fear that, once embarked on this eulogy, the speaker might continue it indefinitely that led Crispin at this point to change the subject by asking Vera if he could show her her room.

'I wonder,' she said when she had seen the room and expressed her approval of it, 'if I could use the telephone. I ought to let my mother know I have arrived.'

'There is a telephone in the library.'

'Oh, thank you,' said Vera. 'Mother,' she said some minutes later, for the Mellingham post office always took its time with calls to London.

The lovely voice of Dame Flora Faye floated over the wire.

'Hullo, my chick. So you've got there. Been down any of the shady walks yet?'

'No. And nothing will happen when I do. Homer's hopeless.'

'What was that you said? Homer hopeless?'

'Absolutely hopeless. We're never going to get any-where.'

'Have patience, my child.'

'I've had all the patience I'm capable of. I tell you, he's hopeless, and I'm not going to waste any more time over him.'

'Then what do you plan to do?'

'I'm going to marry Gerald.'

'The pavement artist! You can't be serious.'

'Yes, I am. He's staying here. I've always been quite fond of Gerald, and he's got his money now. He's rich.'

'Not as rich as Homer.'

'And not as spectacled as Homer. And not as fat as Homer. And not a bore like Homer. Gerald's all right. He only wants moulding. Are you there, mother?'

She asked the question because there had been a prolonged silence at the other end of the wire. Dame Flora had either swooned or was wrestling with her feelings. The latter, it appeared, for she now found speech.

'But has it slipped your mind, honeybunch, that you broke the engagement?'

'I didn't. You did. You misunderstood something I said and went and acted impulsively.'

'On my own? Without your authority?'

'Exactly.'

'You're going to tell him that?'

'As soon as I meet him.'

'It doesn't strike you as a little hard to believe?'

'Not a bit. And anyway when I fling myself into his arms and kiss him...'

'Is that what you have in mind?'

'That's what.'

'Well, lots of luck, my dream girl. You have mother's

best wishes.'

'Thank you, mother.'

'But don't think that I approve. I disapprove heartily.
I don't like that gingerheaded pipsqueak.'

'That's all right, mother dear. You don't have to.'

Chapter Fifteen

In the study Chippendale was showing unmistakeable signs of wishing to be elsewhere. He fidgeted. He licked his lips and stood now on one leg, now on the other. Sherlock Holmes, had he been present, would have deduced that, with ten pounds in his pocket and definite instructions from Jerry West to spend it in revelry, he was thinking of the Goose and Gander and the wines and spirits which its landlord Mr. Hibbs was licensed to sell, and as usual he would have been right.

But though athirst, he did not forget his manners. It was with his customary courtesy that he addressed Barney.

'Would there be anything further, madam?'

'Nothing that occurs to me at the moment. Got a date?'

'In a sense, madam. Mr. West was anxious that I should go to the pub and drink his health.'

'Then don't let me keep you.'

'Thank you, madam.'

'Give my love to the boys in the back room.'

'I will indeed, madam.'

A silence followed his departure. Homer broke it.

'That's a very peculiar butler,' he said.

'As a matter of fact, he's only a synthetic butler. He's really a broker's man. Crips has been having a little trouble with the people who do the repairs, and they sent him down to watch over their interests. But Crips is mailing them a cheque tonight, so we shall be losing him shortly.'

'Oh?' said Homer. This revelation did not seem to have interested him greatly. He had the air of a man whose mind is on other things. 'Well, he's given me an idea.'

'That's good.'

'What he was saying about going and drinking at the Goose and Gander. Do you suppose they would have champagne there?'

'I shouldn't think so.'

'Then I shall have to do what I can with whisky. You see,' said Homer, seeming to feel that if you cannot confide in a sister, in whom can you confide, 'I love Vera Upshaw and I have the most extraordinary difficulty in telling her so. Whenever we are alone together, I find myself talking the merest trivialities. It cannot go on. I must break the spell somehow, and, as I say, that fellow has given me an idea. It has occurred to me that a judicious intake of alcoholic stimulant might do it. It's worth trying, anyway,' said Homer, and he was out of the room at a speed that rivalled Chippendale's.

He left Barney staring after him with bulging eyes and drooping jaw, and it was thus that Crispin, entering at this moment, found her. What with his betrothal and Brotherly Love's victory at a hundred to eight, he had been feeling that everything was for the best in this best of all possible worlds, but the sight of the woman he loved apparently on the verge of having a fit of some kind lowered his high spirits by several degrees, and he uttered a bleat of concern.

'Hullo! I say! Is something wrong, darling? You look like a startled codfish. Suits you, of course. Very becoming. But it gives me the idea that something has happened to upset you. What's the matter, my angel?'

'I've had a shock.'

'Too bad. But it was bound to come. You can't shove policemen into brooks and not get what they call a delayed reaction. It'll pass off. What you need is a drink.'

A strong shudder shook Barney.

'Don't mention that word to me! Homer's gone off to the Goose and Gander to get pie-eyed.'

'Has he, by Jove? Who's Homer?'

'My brother.'

'Of course, yes. I know the chap you mean. He was in here just now, wasn't he? Fellow with horn-rimmed spectacles and a mouse in his bedroom. Why is he going to get pie-eyed?'

'To give him nerve to propose to Vera Upshaw.'

Crispin understood now. As a preliminary to both his breach of promise cases he had had to fortify himself in this manner before being able to express himself.

'Well, that's all right,' he said consolingly, relieved that nothing worse had been responsible for his loved one's agitation, 'Nothing wrong with working himself up, is there?'

'Of course there is. She's a designing Delilah.'

'Why do you say that? She's probably a very nice girl.'

'She isn't! She's a vampire. I spotted it as soon as I saw her. She's after him for his money. She deliberately followed him down here so as to entrap him.'

'Well, you may be right, but even so, aren't you over-looking something?'

'What do you mean?'

'She's bound to refuse him. I wouldn't for the world say anything derogatory about any brother of yours, but let's face it, Homer ... Odd name, that. I wonder why they gave it him. The fact is, parents are apt to lose their heads at the font. Chippendale was telling me about a fellow who got labelled Chingachgook. And look at me, Crispin, and I wouldn't like this to go any further, but I was also christened Lancelot and Gawain, my mother being fond of Tennyson. But where was I?

Oh, yes. I was about to say that Homer, while a sterling chap and full of good stories about mice and all that, isn't an oil painting. You couldn't call him the answer to a maiden's prayer.'

'But he makes a hundred and fifty thousand dollars a year. There isn't a hope that she'll refuse him.'

Crispin saw her point. He appreciated the seriousness of the situation. He mused awhile and was rewarded with an idea.

'Do you know what I think you ought to do?'

'What?'

'Go to the Goose and Gander and reason with him.'

'Oh, Crips, what a help you are!'

'Always glad to lend a hand. Shall I come with you?'

'No. Thanks for the kind offer, but what I have to say to Homer is for his ears alone.'

One of the advantages a sister has when arguing with a brother is that she is under no obligation to be tactful. If she wishes to tell him that he is an idiot and ought to have his head examined, she can do so and, going further, can add that it is a thousand pities that no-one ever thought of smothering him with a pillow in his formative years. Barney did both these things almost immediately after she had entered the saloon bar of the Goose and Gander, and Homer, sipping whisky, said that he did not know what she was talking about.

More than thirty years had passed since in their mutual nursery Barney had settled a dispute with her brother by beating him over the head with a doll which was her constant companion, but she would gladly have done it now, had she had a doll with her. Her thoughts strayed for a moment to a heavy ash tray which was lying on the table, but wiser counsels prevailed, and she confined herself to words.

'You do too know what I'm talking about. I'm talking about you and this gold-digging Vera of yours.'

It is not easy for a man drinking whisky and already

not far from the Plimsoll line to achieve dignity, but Homer made a fair approach to it.

'I must ask you not to speak of Miss Upshaw like that,' he said, stiffening visibly. 'You are merely being absurd. She is incapable of sordid thoughts about money. She is a rare soul who lives on the spiritual plane. One senses it in every line she writes. Read her *Daffodil Days*. Read her *Morning's At Seven*.'

Barney indulged in a brief commination service in which both the works he had named featured largely. She would not, she said, read either of them on a bet.

'Intensely spiritual,' said Homer, now speaking rather thickly and experiencing some difficulty in pronouncing the words. 'Etherial. Refined. Graceful. Light. Dainty. You might say Elfin.'

'All right, I'll take your word for it, but you can't go by that. Half the heels in New York write like angels. Oh, why is it,' said Barney, becoming emotional, 'that you and I are such abysmal saps? It's like some sort of family curse. It seems only yesterday that you were warning me against marrying Wally Claybourne, and I wouldn't listen. I didn't ask myself why a man like Wally, handsome dynamic and the pet of the sporting set, should want to marry a girl whose only charm was her money. I just fell for him with a dull thud. How clear and sensible you were then, and now here you are, all tangled up yourself with a female Wally Clayborne. It's the old business of snakes and rabbits.'

'I beg your pardon?'

'It seems to be a natural law that every rabbit should go out of its class and fall under the spell of a snake. You're a rabbit, I was a rabbit. I was hypnotized by Wally, who, I admit, had everything, including the moral code of a tom cat, and now you've let this Vera Upshaw hypnotize you. Of course she'll marry you if you ask her, but what will there be in it for you? Do you think you'll be able to hold her any more than I was able to hold Wally? She'll be off around the corner, having affairs, before she's digested the wedding cake.'

Homer rose, his dignity impaired by a momentary hiccup. A burst of song from the public bar next door drowned his opening words, compelling him to repeat them.

'I will listen to no more of this,' he said austerely.

'That's your privilege,' said Barney. A gallant fighter, she knew when she was beaten.

'I am going back to the house.'

'All keyed up? All ready to put your fat head in the snake's mouth? Well, I won't come with you. I shall go next door and meet the boys. That singing sounds promising.'

It was with a brother's love for a sister at its lowest ebb that Homer started on his way back to the Hall. Resentment of the subversive stuff to which they had been compelled to listen had turned his ears pink, and his eyes glowed militantly behind their spectacles. Never in his life, he told himself, had he heard such pernicious nonsense as had proceeded from the lips of one whom he had always regarded as fairly well-balanced. Sisters, he supposed, tended to be critical of the objects of their brothers' affections, but to sully a woman like Vera Upshaw with foul innuendos was unpardonable. Even a sister, looking into those clear candid eyes, should have been able to detect the pure white soul that lay beyond them. All that stuff about going around the corner and having affairs. Nauseating.

Not that it had had any effect on his great love. More than ever he yearned to see Vera Upshaw and pour out his heart to her, and the next moment he was given the opportunity of doing so. He had come to the gate and was about to pass through, and there she was, just beyond it. She was linked in a close embrace with a ginger-headed young man in whom he recognized his host's nephew Gerald West, and as he stared dumbfounded she kissed him. And when we say kissed, we use the word in its most exact meaning. It was the sort of kiss which in the days before Hollywood adopted the slogan of Anything Goes would never have been permitted on the silver screen. The Philadelphia censors would have insisted on its being cut by a great many feet.

Homer drew back. He had the odd feeling that somebody had poured a brimming bucket of iced water over him.

Many men in a similar situation would have found their love, seeming so indestructible till then, expiring with a pop, leaving them convinced that they had been vouchsafed a merciful warning and would do well to make a sharp revision of their matrimonial plans. Homer was one of them. It was as though he had made an abrupt recovery from a particularly severe fever. All molten passion a brief moment earlier, he was his calm, cool, collected self again. Homer, the great lover, had vanished without a trace, and in his place stood J. Homer Pyle of Pyle, Wisbeach and Hollister, the corporation lawyer on whom no-one had been able to slip a fast one in the last fifteen years.

The only thing that marred his sense of well-being was the thought that his sister Bernadette was now in a position to say 'I told you so'.

How long he remained there, weighing the sweet against the bitter, he could not have said, but he was still doing this when he perceived an expensive-looking car coming through the gate with Willoughby in the back seat. He sprang into the road and hailed it.

'Hi, Scrope. Just a minute, Scrope. Want to speak to you, Scrope.'

'Yes?' said Willoughby. He spoke grumpily. He had by no means forgiven Homer for his officiousness in the matter of The Girl In Blue. The last thing he desired was to have to interrupt his journey in order to chat with a man capable of putting miniatures in middle drawers.

Homer advanced to the car and clutched it in a firm grip, as if to arrest its progress in the event of it taking it into its head to start again.

'You going to London, Scrope?'

'Yes.'

'Can you give me a lift?'

'I suppose so,' said Willoughby, still grumpy. 'Why do you want to go to London?'

It would have been possible for Homer to say that he had had a cable from America which made his immediate presence in the metropolis imperative, but he decided that the truth from one man of the world to another man of the world would carry more weight.

'There's a woman here I want to avoid,' he said.

He could not have framed a sentence more calculated to win Willoughby's sympathy. That sturdy bachelor never turned a deaf ear to appeals from men desirous of avoiding women. He had been doing it himself for years and considered it the foundation stone on which the good life should be based.

'Jump in,' he said, and Homer jumped in.

'Tell me all about it,' he said, and Homer told him all about it.

'If I were you,' said Willoughby, the narrative concluded, 'I'd take the next plane back to New York. Never mind about your luggage. Leave it behind,' said Willoughby, and Homer said that the same idea had occurred to him.

2

Jerry was pacing to and fro near the gate. He was feeling shaken, but happy to have placed his relations with Vera Upshaw on a satisfactory basis. It had not been easy to detach her from his person and explain to her without being abrupt that his affections were engaged elsewhere and that her suggestion that everything between them should be just as it was before, Gerald dear, was not to be considered for an instant, but he had managed it. The thought of Jane had lent him eloquence, and even without telling her that he would greatly prefer to be dead in a ditch than married to her he had been able to make himself clear.

She had not been pleased, but dudgeon in the circumstances was only to be expected, and a little dudgeon, he told himself, never did anyone any harm. The thing to fix the mind on was that she had left him and he was alone again, free to meditate on Jane, undisturbed.

So intently was he doing this that it was only when a motor horn tooted immediately behind him, causing him to skip like the high hills, that he became aware that she had returned from her trip to London. She was looking radiant at the wheel of the car with which the bounty of Scrope, Ashby and Pemberton had provided her, and he thought, as he had so often thought before, that there was something about her that made all other girls of his acquaintance seem like battered repaints. He hastened to the window and poked his head in.

Their conversation opened on perhaps a pedestrian note.

'Hullo,' he said.

'Hi,' she replied.

'So you're back.'

'Yes, I'm back!'

'Did you have a nice drive?'

'Terrific.'

'Tired?'

'Not a bit.'

'Did you see the lawyer?'

'Yes, I saw him. His name's Stoganbuhler.'

'Well, sooner him than me.'

There was a momentary silence. Then Jane said:

'Will I what?' and when Jerry asked her to clarify the

question, she said Certainly.

'When I left, we were talking of this and that and you said "Jane, will you?", and before you could proceed further Chippendale came butting in. So now, devoured by curiosity, I ask Will I what?'

'Marry me. Be my wife. Team up.'

'Oh, was that it? Need you ask?'

'I thought I'd better. Will you, Jane?'

'Of course I will. I can hardly wait. So now what you do is climb in and kiss me, don't you think?'

'It was just what I was planning to do.'

'But I wish you weren't going to do it with your face all over lipstick.'

'Is it?'

'Smothered.'

'I had better explain.'

'I think so. If you can.'

'That was a girl I used to be engaged to. She broke it off, and wanted it to be on again. She made a sudden dive for me. I ought to have uppercut her as she bored in, but I missed my chance. However, everything is all right. I told her I was engaged to you.'

'But you weren't.'

'I may have anticipated a little, but I am now, aren't I?'

'You certainly are.'

'Gosh, how happy we're going to be.'

'There won't be any more of your ex-fiancées dropping in and kissing you?'

'No, that's the lot.'

'Good. One likes to know.'

It was some time later that Jane, when able to speak, said 'Jerry', and Jerry, who had been murmuring incoherently, said 'Yes?'

'There's one little thing I ought to tell you.'

'I know it.'

'About my money?'

'Yes. Uncle Bill turned up just now with the story.'

'And don't you mind?'

'Not if you don't.'

'I'm delighted. When Stoganbuhler broke the news, I felt like laughing my head off. It would only have come between us.'

'Nothing could ever come between us.'

'What's money?'

'Exactly.'

'Dross, wouldn't you call it?'.

'Just the word.'

'Who wants money if they've got G. G. F. West? Though I'm afraid we shall be awfully hard up. I've got to give your uncle all he lent me for this car and my other extravagances. I've been spending a fortune. Like a drunken sailor, as he said. You won't mind love in a cottage, will you, or in a small flat somewhere?'

'We can do better than that. Uncle Bill has terminated the trust, and I'm loaded. Loaded enough, anyway. Any time you want a little dross, ask me.'

'Jerry! How wonderful.'

'Not too bad, I agree.'

'Oh, Jerry!' said Jane.

'Oh, Jane!' said Jerry.

Odd, he reflected, how things turn out. If some unknown sadist had not selected him for jury duty, chuckling at the thought of how it was going to disorganize his working day, he would never have known that Jane existed. Giving credit where credit was due, he saw in the miracle of their meeting one more proof of his guardian angel's efficiency. When that magician undertook a job, he certainly gave service.

In the intervals of kissing Jane he pondered on his guardian angel. For some reason he pictured him as smallish with one of those rather sharp faces. Horn-rimmed spectacles? Yes, probably horn-rimmed spectacles and a nervous bustling manner, the sort of fellow who would have made a good confidential secretary to a big financier.

What had he done to deserve such a helper? Not much, that he could see. Still, there it was, and he could at least be grateful.

3

Two persons of opposite sexes cannot sit embracing in a car in a public place like the driveway of Mellingham Hall for long without being seen, and Barney and Chippendale, returning from the Goose and Gander, got a good view of Jane and Jerry some minutes later. They were just in time, for as they entered the gate the car drove off.

'Going to be married, those two, wouldn't you think?' said Chippendale, and Barney replied that if they weren't, they certainly ought to be, adding that they appeared to have got off to a good start.

'Mr. West and his girl friend,' said Chippendale.

'Nice fellow, Mr. West.'

'Couldn't be nicer.'

'I'd have liked to stay on here and see more of him.'

'You're leaving us?'

'Tomorrow,' said Chippendale. He heaved a sigh. 'That's the worst of being a broker's man. You didn't know I was one, did you?'

'Yes, Mr. Scrope told me. Drawback to being a broker's man, you were saying?'

'What I had in mind was, you come to a house, get all comfortable, make nice friends, and then all of a sudden you have to leave. You might call me a bird of passage.'

'A bird of some kind, certainly.'

'Sort of sad.'

'But think how glad everybody will be to see you go.'

'Something in that,' said Chippendale, brightening.

'Always try to put yourself in the other fellow's place. You're one of those guys who can make a party just by leaving it. It's a great gift.'

'I see what you mean.'

'You remember that old song, Spread a little happiness. Let's sing it, shall we?'

'Okay. I don't recall the words too well. I'll have to go tum-tum-tum a bit.'

'Tum-tum-tum to your heart's content. It's the spirit that matters. Ready?'

'I'm ready.'

'Then let's get down to it.'

They got down to it.